Stuck
Together

Stuck
Together

Stories from a Small Town

Raymond N. Armstrong

iUniverse, Inc.
New York Bloomington

Stuck Together
Stories from a Small Town

iUniverse books may be ordered through booksellers or by contacting:

iUniverse
1663 Liberty Drive
Bloomington, IN 47403
www.iuniverse.com
1-800-Authors (1-800-288-4677)

Because of the dynamic nature of the Internet, any Web addresses or links contained in this book may have changed since publication and may no longer be valid. This is a work of fiction. All of the characters, names, incidents, organizations, and dialogue in this novel are either the products of the author's imagination or are used fictitiously.

ISBN: 978-1-4401-7591-6 (pbk)
ISBN: 978-1-4401-7592-3 (ebk)

Printed in the United States of America
iUniverse rev. date: 9/24/2009

"The worst thing about living in a small town is, everybody knows your business. The best thing about living in a small town is, everybody knows your business."

-Marcia Powell

The Fire Chief's Wife

In memory of my parents,

Robert and Rachel Armstrong,

who grew up in small Indiana towns.

Acknowledgements

I owe a great deal to the dozens of people I've talked with over fifty years who have lived in small towns. Their stories of local characters and small town customs have informed and inspired these fictional tales of a town that might have been—and in many places still exists. Some of the characters are composites of real persons; some are entirely fictional. No single town is intended as the model for Thornburg, Indiana, but many have contributed to its form and patterns. They share family values, community solidarity, and a too-close familiarity with one another's problems and relationships. This, as the Fire Chief's wife has said, is both good and bad. My own experience of living in a small town has borne that out.

Particular thanks are due Hannah Jones, who created the map of Thornburg, Indiana, and Shaun Lieberman, who created the interactive website. For more details on the places and characters in these stories, go to ThornburgIndiana@comcast.net.

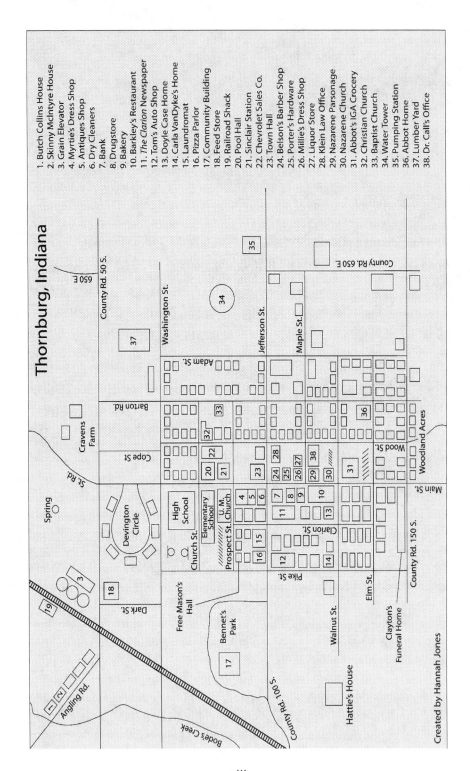

Thornburg, Indiana

1. Butch Collins House
2. Skinny McIntyre House
3. Grain Elevator
4. Myrtie's Dress Shop
5. Antiques Shop
6. Dry Cleaners
7. Bank
8. Drugstore
9. Bakery
10. Barkley's Restaurant
11. *The Clarion* Newspaper
12. Tom's Auto Shop
13. Doyle Case Home
14. Carla VanDyke's Home
15. Laundromat
16. Pizza Parlor
17. Community Building
18. Feed Store
19. Railroad Shack
20. Pool Hall
21. Sinclair Station
22. Chevrolet Sales Co.
23. Town Hall
24. Belson's Barber Shop
25. Porter's Hardware
26. Millie's Dress Shop
27. Liquor Store
28. Klein Law Office
29. Nazarene Parsonage
30. Nazarene Church
31. Abbot's IGA Grocery
32. Christian Church
33. Baptist Church
34. Water Tower
35. Pumping Station
36. Abbot Home
37. Lumber Yard
38. Dr. Call's Office

Created by Hannah Jones

Contents

Joe Bennett

Dirty, stooped, shambling, he groped his way along Main Street to Spencer's bakery. He had searched the sidewalks and gutters for coins, and now he had enough to buy a doughnut. The bakery shared a wall with the drugstore. Shuffling in, he laid six pennies on the counter. A lady in white, waxed paper in hand, put a doughnut into a white sack and handed it to Joe Bennett, the town tramp. The loner. The outcast who lived in an abandoned barn across a field west of town.

Outside, he moved to the public fountain on the corner, a large porcelain basin with a brass spout in its center bubbling clear, cold water. Thornburg, Indiana, was known for its good water. A spring at the north end of town, down a slope toward the creek, provided an endless supply. People brought trunkfuls of water jugs to fill and take home for coffee and drinking.

Joe Bennett stood by the fountain and ate his doughnut while the town watched. Children had been taught to keep their distance from him. So far as anyone knew, he had never bothered a child. But why take chances? A few stood across the street and stared as crumbs dropped into the basin. He finished eating, drank from the fountain, wiped his mouth on his ragged sleeve, and shuffled on down the street.

Many had witnessed this ritual over the more than sixty years Joe had lived in the community. His mother had died in childbirth. The boy had pretty much raised himself. The truant officer saw to it that he attended first and second grades, but then it became too time consuming to find him and transport him from his drunken father's hovel to the school. Eventually he was declared mentally incompetent and allowed to roam the streets, scavenging whatever he could from the alleys of the town and the goodness of people's hearts.

Older residents had known his father, Estey. In earlier years Estey had been a harness-maker, then liquor claimed him. Several folks had witnessed his treatment of his son in times of drunkenness: beating the boy until bruises colored his face and arms for a week. This lasted well into Joe's teen years.

Estey lost his home when he could no longer pay the rent. He moved into the empty barn, where he was found late one night with his throat cut. Mahlon Parker, the owner of the barn, was arrested. He had been overheard once saying to Estey,

"You beat that boy one more time, and you'll answer to me."

But he was out of town when Estey was killed, and for lack of evidence he never came to trial. Nevertheless, he was shunned by the town population. In a few months he moved away without saying good-bye to anyone.

Joe was wandering the alleys of town when the constable told him of his father's death. He stood still a long time, looking toward the field and the barn, and said nothing. The constable patted him on the shoulder and said he was sorry, then left him. Joe stayed on in the barn. Nobody objected.

He seldom ate a whole meal, and never in a house. Sometimes a housewife would give him a sandwich, and he would sit on the back step and eat it. No one ever invited him to share a cup of coffee in a restaurant. No one conversed with him.

John Magnuson, the township trustee, had tried on several occasions to help Joe find a job, but it came to nothing. No one would hire him unless he bathed and came to work on time. Those requirements seemed beyond Joe's ability to fulfill.

"He's a ragpicker," Ed Porter said. "That's all he'll ever be. Some folks just don't have what it takes to make it in this world, and Joe's one of 'em. His father was the same way."

The town hardly knew how to feel about Joe. He seemed harmless enough, walking the alleys of town carrying discarded household items under his arm. Sometimes he hauled a gunnysack on his back, filled with treasures he gleaned from trash cans and open sheds along the backyards. No one complained, because he never took anything useful. Empty containers, bottles, broken appliances, cast-off household goods and clothing were his stock-in-trade. People seemed to think of Joe as performing a service to the community, carrying off the things that the town trash collector would have to dispose of were it not for Joe. What he did with those things was anyone's guess.

On winter nights some of the more compassionate souls in town lay in bed and wondered where Joe was sleeping. The old barn he lived in was visibly full of holes where the icy wind must be whistling through. No one ever saw smoke coming from the openings, so he must not have had a fire. Maybe he crawled under the straw to keep warm. He certainly wore enough clothes: layers of old suits, work pants, jackets, and a gray felt hat so old it had mold along the brim. He was never without it. His hair descended from under it, gray and greasy.

In warm weather Joe simply discarded a few layers. He changed his shoes as he found replacements among the piles of personal jetsam stacked in heaps along the alleys. Sometimes folks spoke pleasantly to him, sometimes they did not. It was all the same to him. He had nothing to say in return. In later years, folks said they couldn't remember ever hearing his voice. His face seemed so nondescript that few could recall it. He was a generic person, without distinction in any way except filth. His odor lingered in the establishments he entered. Parents would draw their children away from him, whispering to them that Joe was not the kind of person they should be around.

After he had eaten his doughnut, no one drank from the fountain until the town maintenance men cleaned it. No one stood near him on the streets or in the shops. No one ever went to his barn across the unmown field where a narrow path revealed his habitual way. He had no friends in any true sense of the word. Thornburg was a town of tolerant citizens who lived and let live. Joe seemed oblivious to the taunts of teenage boys and the glances of people on the streets. He made no more impression on the town's consciousness than did the silver maples that lined the sidewalks, or the weekly passage of the Pennsylvania Railroad's freight cars.

The town assumed Joe Bennett.

For that reason, I suppose, it was a couple of weeks before anyone realized that Joe had not been seen for a while. Someone mentioned it to John Magnuson in late December. He promised to look into the matter. In early January, he began to inquire at Joe's usual haunts: the bakery, the filling station where Joe sometimes bought a Coke, the bank where he was often seen sitting on the steps, staring into his own private distance. No one had seen him since before Christmas. The Women's Missionary Society at the Baptist Church had given him a box of candy and some cookies on the street. That was his last appearance.

A heavy snow fell on the first day of the year, followed by sub-zero temperatures. Folks assumed Joe was staying put until the weather warmed a bit.

"I suppose a couple of us ought to go out to his barn," John said to Ted Bates, the town marshal, one afternoon. "He might be sick or something."

"I'm sure he needs food," Ted said. The marshal was a tall, ruggedly handsome man, well suited to his job. Some of the men in town who knew him best kidded him about being single, but he only answered, "I guess I just never found the right woman." He was a good marshal. The town knew itself fortunate to have him. Several deputies had served under him over the years, but he was the dependable figure of law in Thornburg.

John Magnuson was a family man, a former realtor and tax accountant, with three grown children and seven grandchildren. John took his job seriously, dispensing public funds to needy families. At Christmas he organized a meal for folks who lived alone or otherwise might be denied a Christmas dinner. It was usually held in one of the church dining rooms. John always made it a point to invite Joe Bennett, but Joe never came.

Ted picked up John in the police car the next morning, and the two men drove out to the field where Joe's barn stood. Parking on the road, they plodded through the snow to the door. It had been frozen partly open. Squeezing through, they could see nothing until Ted switched on his flashlight.

The scene astonished them. In orderly rows, on shelves of planks on overturned buckets and stacked in neat groups throughout the barn lay the waste of sixty years of the town's history. Hundreds of tobacco cans, fruit jars, china plates and cups that didn't match, castoff toys, appliances, and books of every kind filled the barn. Joe had collected and stored all the rejects of a town that outgrew its past and moved on. He had kept what people declared useless, things that now appeared all over the state in antique shops at high prices. Old hurricane lamps, glassware, jewelry, tools, and other items too numerous to mention lined the walls of the barn and filled the narrow aisles Joe had made of boxes. He had wrapped many things in old rugs, bedspreads, and sheets. The boxes were full of newspapers, magazines, and snapshots of people and places long forgotten. The barn might have been a time capsule, boxed and buried for posterity.

John and Ted looked in every corner, but Joe was not to be found. They called his name. No answer. The only response was the echo of their voices from copper wash boilers, tin cocoa cans, wash tubs, and ewers once used in bedrooms to wash before retiring. The men moved an ancient wooden washing machine, a one-cylinder Maytag engine, several parts of a 1916 Model T Ford, and a dressing mirror still intact except for a broken leg. Ted shined the flashlight into every available space, but Joe was not there.

Returning to town, they put out the word that Joe was missing, and anyone who knew anything of his whereabouts should tell the marshal. A search through county records revealed that Mahlon Parker had died many years before, leaving no heirs. Which meant that if Joe could not be found, or if he were found dead, the property, the barn, and everything in it belonged to the town.

John was not for doing anything until Joe was found, so a general search was initiated. Several teenage boys joined in the hunt, expecting (hoping?) to find Joe hanging from a tree in the woods. They bundled up and spread out through the thicket northwest of town. Other residents searched their garages. Men walked the creek bank in both directions, fearing he might have fallen through the ice.

Two of them walked the railroad track north as far as Two-mile Road, but no Joe. On the way back, they noticed that the switchman's shack door was unbolted and partly open. They peered inside. There on the floor lay Joe Bennett in a fetal position, his ragged coat pulled over his head in a last effort to survive the cold. One of the men knelt beside him and felt for a pulse.

"He's dead. Frozen stiff."

"Musta got caught out in the snow and tried to get back to his barn."

"Poor old guy. That's no way to go."

They stood in silence a few minutes. Then, leaving Joe there, they closed the door carefully, dropped the bolt through the hasp, and trudged back to town to tell the marshal.

Ted called Melvin Clayton, the local undertaker, and asked him to pick up Joe's body. Then he drove out to the barn and put a padlock on the door.

Melvin told John Magnuson some days later that when he undressed Joe to wash him, the hair on Joe's body had grown through his long underwear. Melvin had to cut it off with a straight razor. Joe was so dirty that Melvin put him through a series of soakings to get him clean enough to bury.

"And look at this." He handed John a heavy brown pocketknife with wooden scales.

John turned it over in his hand. "Was this his?"

"It was in his pants pocket."

John pried open the rusty blade. "It's a hawk billed knife. Farmers often carry 'em. My Dad had one."

He looked up at Melvin. "Would a harness-maker use one of these?"

"Well it must have been his father's," Melvin said. "Look at the initials carved on the side."

Two letters, still legible in spite of the years, had been scratched into the wood: "EB."

"The only thing his father left him, I suppose," John observed. "It'd make a nasty weapon, wouldn't it?"

They looked at each other a moment and said nothing.

"What should I do with it?"

"Just put it back in his pocket," John said.

The town paid for the funeral. Several folks attended, filing past the casket to view the face that was largely a mystery to them. They had never seen it clean or shaven. Joe seemed to be at peace, his hair neatly cut, his face smooth except for the wrinkles of age. Melvin had dressed him in simple clothes: a clean blue shirt and dark blue trousers.

Harry Corman, the Baptist pastor, read some scripture about "little ones" entering the Kingdom of God and said some nice things about Joe. Then a small retinue of cars escorted Joe to the cemetery west of town, where he was buried beside his parents.

"That's the first time I ever really knew what he looked like," Leona Abbot said as they left the cemetery.

"He really wasn't all that bad looking," her husband observed. "First time I ever saw his hair cut. Harvey Wilcomb says he looked a lot like his father."

"I never knew his father," she answered. "But then, I never really knew Joe, either. I don't suppose anybody did."

Spring came before anyone did anything about Joe's barn. Word had got out that it contained "slews of stuff you just wouldn't believe," as Mrs. Billings put it. She and her husband had borrowed the key to the padlock from Marshal Bates and trekked out to the barn when the weather warmed and the ground dried a bit.

"Why, there's a fortune in antiques out there!" she told the marshal.

Acting on her authority as secretary of the town board, she contacted an antiques dealer in Ohio, who came over one afternoon and looked up the marshal.

"Had a call from a Mrs. Billings about a barn full of antiques," he said. "Ya mind if I take a look at it? Just might be there's a major auction possible. Pays to look into it."

Ted drove him out to the barn. The man looked everything over.

"We'd have to talk with the town council," the marshal told him. "We couldn't do anything without their say-so."

"Well, here's my card. Let me know. I just think you got yerself a heck of a good deal out there. That's collectible stuff, y'know." And he went back to Ohio.

The next town council meeting took up the subject of Joe's barn. Mrs. Sorley, whose house was filled with antiques, proposed an auction of the items Joe had collected over half a century.

"The town could use the money," she pointed out. "No sense in it just layin' out there rotting."

"Where would we hold it?" someone asked.

"Well, when the weather warms up enough, we could mow that field and just have it there," someone else proposed.

And so it was decided.

Over the next few weeks, several volunteers sorted the things in the barn, ready for the auction. Two men with mowing machines cut the weeds that in some places stood shoulder high, then raked and mowed the field again. An announcement was sent to the area newspapers, handbills were distributed in the neighboring towns, and an auction of "The Joseph Bennett Estate" was declared for May 7, 1949, at nine o'clock in the morning.

It was a Saturday; the weather was perfect, and folks came from miles around. The itemization had been extensive in the papers. Cars parked along the road and in the field to the south. The man from Ohio launched into his auctioneering. He was a good choice; he knew his business well.

The women of the Methodist Church set up a lunch tent: Sloppy Joes, potato salad, baked beans, and twelve kinds of pie were the menu—all for $2.00. Several folks threw in an extra dollar and ate an extra piece of pie. Lemonade, iced tea, and coffee were included.

Bidding was brisk. Some of the prices people paid for Joe's treasures astonished others. By suppertime most of the barn was empty, hauled away in pickups, trailers, and automobile trunks, even carried by hand back into the houses from which those same items had been evicted decades ago. Several men swept the barn and closed the door, and the Joe Bennett era was over.

"Eighteen thousand four hundred and sixty dollars," John Magnuson said at the supper table. "Would you believe it?"

"Who'd a thought there was that much stuff in town?" his wife said.

"Who'd a thought it was worth anything?" John responded. "But I guess time makes everything valuable."

At the next town council meeting the big question was what to do with the money.

"It don't rightly belong to us," said Mr. Wheatley. "We throwed that stuff away years ago."

"Seems to me it belongs to the whole community," Mrs. Sorley said. "After all, it was our stuff to begin with."

After much discussion and several long silences, Elnora Devington, a long-time widow with no children, suggested, "Why don't we use it to build a park? We don't have any decent place for the children to play.

If we mowed that field and put in swings and slides, maybe a merry-go-round, the children would have a wonderful place to play."

Her husband, Russell, had owned and operated the canning factory two miles north of town during the 1930s. He died suddenly one evening of a heart attack in his early forties. The foreman and Mrs. Devington tried to keep the enterprise going, but tomato farming proved too labor intensive. When the war started, she closed the plant. It stood empty until after the war, when she sold it to Carnie Woodson. He tore down the buildings and farmed the land.

Mrs. Devington bought the property just north of the high school and engaged a contractor to build several houses on a horseshoe drive. She sold her former home at Elm and Main Streets and moved into the first house on Devington Circle. But it was a lonely house. If there was a park nearby, she could spend time with children and their parents. It seemed to her like a perfect solution. The town council thought so too.

The vote was unanimous: the field became "Bennett's Park." The old barn, structurally sound–its timbers were entire tree trunks–was made into a community building. Men from town donated their labor and skill, and by the middle of June it was finished. Children played on the playground, families had picnics there, and couples walked out to the park on summer evenings to sit on the benches and watch the sun set. Clubs held meetings in the building. Men pitched horseshoes beyond the swings and slides. Bennett's Park became the focal point of the community's leisure hours.

Mrs. Devington spent her summer days talking with the children, pushing them on the swings and catching them at the bottom of the slide. She found many friends among the parents who brought them there. She had not been so happy in many years.

When Christmas came around that year, the Trustee's office held the dinner in the community building. At least a hundred people showed up. Groups of women from the churches outdid themselves, bringing casseroles, salads, and desserts to complement the turkey and ham provided by the town. Eggnog, hot cider, and coffee washed down the doughnuts, pies, and cakes. Homemade candies and cookies all decorated in red and green sprinkles overflowed their Christmas paper plates. A few folks who hadn't had a square meal in weeks stuffed themselves to the limit.

A huge Christmas tree was stacked beneath with packages that John Magnuson, dressed in a Santa Claus coat and hat, distributed to the children. Some boxes contained coats, hats, and mittens for kids in town who would otherwise have gone without.

A trio from Cranfield came with a violin, a banjo, and a square dance caller. Folks who had not danced in many years took the floor in a scene reminiscent of Fezziwig's Ball. It was the best Christmas celebration the town had had in anyone's memory.

"Here's to Joe Bennett!" called John Magnuson, raising his cup of cider after the dancing.

"To Joe!" the crowd echoed, and drank to his memory.

"I just wish he could be here," Helen Magnuson said.

"Why's that?" asked John.

"He could have all the doughnuts he wanted."

A Leftover Boy

On a warm evening in the middle of June, Ed Porter propped open the door to his hardware store. He and Myron Dunwiddie and John Abbot sat inside, watching the people on Main Street and talking about how the "gov'ment" ought to be run. One of the three television sets in town glowed and flickered in the window of the store, a Muntz on which fuzzy images of Ted Mack's Original Amateur Hour appeared as if in a snowstorm. The Old Gold Cigarette box danced in wavy lines across the screen. Ed had turned down the sound in order to talk.

A boy in his teen years walked by outside, his hair down to the neck of his T-shirt, his baggy jeans worn through at the knees and the cuffs turned up.

"Whose boy is that, anyway?" Myron asked.

"That boy belongs to about fifteen of the best men around Cranfield," Ed said. The other two chuckled knowingly.

"Who's his mother? She live here in town?"

"Used to. But she moved away ten or twelve years ago. I don't remember where. Her husband disappeared before that. The boy lives with his sister and her husband out beyond the track."

"That row o' hovels on the anglin' road?"

"Down at the end of those. Y'don't see much of that pair. He works part-time at the elevator. Rest o' the time I think he does odd jobs—light hauling, stuff like that. They don't have much."

Ed thought a moment then said, "Name's Johnson, I think."

"That boy was over at the house with my boys one day last week," John said. "I could hear 'em talkin' up in the boys' room. I don't know what it was about, but I don't like 'em havin' secrets. I asked 'em what they were up to, but they just said, 'Oh, nothin',' and went on out. Sometimes I don't know what to do with 'em. Leona don't seem to worry about 'em as much as I do."

"What's the kid's name?" Myron asked.

"All I ever heard him called was Butch," Ed said. "I don't know if he has a last name or not."

"It ain't good for him to be runnin' the streets like that," Myron said.

"Boys that age is awful hard to control," Ed said. "I know when mine was teenagers, we used to have some pretty serious talks. But their mother and I stuck together on it, and we managed to get 'em to maturity—with the help of God and the rest of the town. They didn't turn out too bad, I reckon."

"No, you got no worries with your children, Ed," John agreed. "They're fine men and women—all four of 'em."

"I guess I oughta thank my lucky stars we had all girls," said Myron. "They seem easier to raise. Anyway, the wife does most of the raisin'. I just pay the bills."

This was greeted with laughter and general agreement.

The dusk turned to twilight. Ed got up, took the brick away from the door, and stubbed out his cigar in the ashtray.

"Well, Fellas, I think I'll call it a day."

"Yep, it's about suppertime," John said. He and Myron helped close the store.

When John got home, he found his wife in the kitchen, just taking a casserole from the oven.

"The boys in?" he asked.

"Upstairs," his wife answered. Leona was a quiet woman in her mid-forties. She set the hot casserole on one of the burners of the stove. "You been up at Ed's?"

"Yep. Ed thinks we're in for some rain this weekend. Hope he's right."

"You want to tell the boys supper's ready?"

John went upstairs and knocked on the boys' door, then opened it. The twins were lying on their beds reading comic books. They even adopted the same posture: belly down and legs bent back over their thighs.

"Supper's on the table," their father said.

"All right!"

They followed their father downstairs. Grace was said and the dishes passed in silence. Leona spooned the casserole onto the plates.

After a few moments John asked, "Say, what's that boy's name that runs around with you two—Butch something?"

"Collins," James answered in the midst of chewing.

"His first name is Francis, but he hates it," Junior said. "We just call him Butch. Why?"

"Just wondered. Saw him uptown this evening. None of us knew who he was."

The family continued to eat, and the subject was dropped.

After supper the boys went back up to their room. John went into the living room. When his wife had finished washing the dishes she joined him. He put down his newspaper and looked up.

"You know, I don't like our boys running around with that Collins kid. We know almost nothing about him or his family. He always looks kinda sullen or—I don't know–mad about somethin' all the time."

"Well, he's practically an orphan," Leona said. "I don't suppose he has much to be happy about." She sat beside him and took up her sewing.

"Well, I just wish the boys would find somebody a little higher class to run with," John said. "He could be a bad influence on 'em."

"Don't you think it's possible our boys could be a *good* influence on him?" Leona suggested. She smiled at her husband.

"I hope so," he said. "All the same, I intend to keep an eye on 'em this summer. Summer's a time for boys to get in trouble. I might put 'em to work at the store again."

"Well, Dear, they worked all last summer in the store. I can't see what it hurts for them have a little time to themselves before their senior year."

"Workin' in a grocery is good experience," John said. "They need to learn how to work, instead of layin' around all day readin' comic books."

"Well, if that's the way you feel about it, I guess they could work part-time. I just think it's good for boys to have time for fishing and baseball and so on. They'll be grown and gone before we know it, and then we'll be wishing they were back home."

"Not me," John said. "I'm hopin' they'll get married and move away. Costs a fortune to feed boys."

She smiled at him. "Now, you don't mean that."

On a sweltering Friday evening of the next week, the twins and Butch "borrowed" an army surplus Jeep from Butch's brother-in-law, who had gone to bed early, and took a ride in the country. They drove past Luther Cravens's farm on the state road north of town, then turned east onto the gravel road that ran along a field where Luther's Holstein cows had gathered in a corner. Butch stopped the Jeep by the cows. They got to their feet and stared at the boys.

James leaned out of the Jeep and began a low, soft "mooing" sound. The herd began to stir nervously. Butch turned the Jeep around and started driving slowly back along the road beside the fence. The twins continued "mooing" at the cows as the Jeep picked up speed. The herd followed them, loping along the fence.

At the corner of the field near the highway, Butch turned again and started back. The cows followed, running now and "mooing" as they ran. This scenario occupied most of an hour, running back and forth along the fence until the cows were too tired to keep it up. The boys laughed at this great fun. Butch drove the boys to a corner near their house, where he let them out to walk home.

The next morning Luther Cravens was talking with some of the men at the grain elevator, complaining that his cows had "gone dry overnight."

"I didn't get enough milk this morning to fill a bucket," Luther said. "It's like they was on strike or somethin'."

"It's this heat," one of the other men said. "Our chickens ain't layin' either."

"Well, if it don't let up soon, I'll go broke," Luther said. "I never seen nothin' like it."

Word eventually got back to the boys, who congratulated themselves on a good prank and immediately made plans to outdo it.

"I got an idea," Junior said. "I heard about it from a kid at camp last summer." He outlined the plan, and the other two agreed that it would be even better than dry cows.

On the first Wednesday night in July, the three of them left a Fourth-of-July party early—it was held at a home east of the school—and walked up Barton Road that teed at County Road 50 S, the southern border of Luther Cravens's farm. Climbing the fence, they crept across the darkened field of wheat stubble to Luther's barn. An old barn door lay among the outbuildings. A stack of railroad ties that Luther had procured for building a trench silo stood nearby.

"Perfect!" James exclaimed. They went looking for a cow.

"She's gotta be gentle," Junior said. "We don't want one that's gonna thrash around."

They looked over the herd in a corner of the adjoining field and picked out the one with the most white on her.

"She looks gentle," Junior said. "Just go up and put this rope around her neck, James, then lead her out the gate."

"Why don't you go? You got the rope," James said.

"Well, here. Take it. Now go! Go on!"

"Chicken!" said James as he took the rope.

Butch and Junior watched from the gate, while James walked as casually as he could toward the cows, holding an ear of corn in his extended hand. The herd stood up as he approached. He spoke quietly to them, trying to reassure them. One or two stretched their necks in his direction. Some took a step or two toward him. He stopped, rope in hand, and waited until the white cow was standing still. He simply walked up to her and gently put the lasso around her neck.

Grinning over his shoulder at the boys, he began to walk slowly backward toward the gate, coaxing the cow with soft words. She followed him as though he were Luther leading her to the barn. Junior and Butch opened the gate, and James led her out.

They took the cow to the barn door they had found and tethered her to an iron ring, once part of its locking mechanism. She stood obediently on the door, munching the corn, while the boys dragged over a railroad tie. It took all three of them to lift one edge of the door enough to slide the tie under. The cow shifted nervously; the boys waited to see what she would do.

"Get her some hay," Butch said. Junior found a bale of hay in the barn and dragged it to the door, placing it directly in front of the cow.

"We're gonna need a jack or somethin' to lift the other side," James said. "She's too heavy for us."

They went into the barn and found a tractor jack. Dragging it back to the tethered cow, they lifted the opposite side with a pry bar and slid the jack under. Then it was a simple matter of jacking up the door and sliding in another railroad tie. This process continued for the next hour or more, crisscrossing the railroad ties until the cow was now about ten feet off the ground, patiently chewing her cud.

"We sure picked the right cow," Junior said. "She'll be there 'til morning."

Laughing with glee at their ingenious prank, they crossed the wheat stubble once more, climbed the fence, and parted at the county road for their separate homes.

The next morning Luther Cravens stalked into the marshal's office.

"I'm tellin' you, Marshal, somebody's gonna get shot! Now I mean it! I ain't gonna put up with much more." He banged his fist on the marshal's desk. "Somebody put one o' my cows on a platform ten feet in the air last night, and I intend to find out who it was and see that they're punished."

"Now Luther," Marshal Bates said, trying to calm him, "it was probably just a prank. I've already heard about it. Nobody got hurt, and you got your cow down, didn't you? She's all right, isn't she?"

"Well, it took me and two others—Paul Manning and Benny Jones—to get 'er down. I'm tellin' you, if you don't do somethin' about it, I'm gonna take the law into my own hands!"

"Now Luther, you leave it up to me. I'll find out what's going on and put a stop to it. You just go on home and try to forget it. I'll let you know when I find out something."

Luther left the marshal's office in a fume. Ted dialed the high school and asked for the principal, Marlin Parsons.

"Marlin, this is Ted Bates. We've had a small incident out at the Cravens farm involving a cow. I thought you might have heard some scuttlebutt about it."

"A cow, you say? No, I haven't. What happened to the cow?"

"Well, Luther was in here just now saying he found one of his cows tied up on a barn door"—here Ted chuckled into the phone—"about ten feet up in the air. Seems whoever did it used a bunch of railroad ties to build a rack underneath and left her high and dry."

"No, I haven't heard a word about it," Parsons said. "But I'll ask around. Maybe somebody'll know something. *Ten feet in the air!*"

"That's what he said. Sounds like a bunch of boys to me, wouldn't you say?"

"Well, I can remember some things we did when I was a boy," Parsons said. "But I don't remember being that creative." Both men laughed, and Ted hung up the phone.

He made some inquiries that day and found that there had been a party at a girl's home on the evening in question. But no one he asked could offer any information. The twins and Butch kept quiet about it, which was the hardest part of all. They enjoyed the notoriety in silence and discussed what they could do next to top this brilliant performance.

A few weeks passed, and what with working in their father's grocery and having to help paint the fence at home, the Abbot twins were kept too busy to plan more creative stunts to aggravate Luther Cravens. Butch spent his time at the arcade on Pike Street behind the pizza parlor, or "crawdaddin," as he called it, in Bode's Creek.

Meanwhile, Luther Cravens had had enough. He told the marshal he had decided to sell his farm and move to Florida.

"Since my wife died, I've tried to make a go of it, you know, but my heart ain't in it. We lost our only son in the war. Now it don't seem to matter if I farm or not. Ain't no one to do it for anymore, just me."

"Well, Luther," Ted said, "I'd hate to see you go. Lots of folks would. You're part of us. Wasn't that your father's farm before you?"

"Yep. I grew up on that farm," Luther said, "but it ain't home no more. I get too lonely just plantin' and harvestin' for no one but myself. Last week I found myself talkin' to the barn cats like they was human. If I don't get out o' here soon, I think I'll go completely crazy."

"Well, think it over, Luther," Ted said. "You don't want to do something hasty and regret it later."

Cravens left the marshal's office, and Ted walked down the street to the hardware store. Ed Porter was in the back making a key for a customer. Ted waited until he finished.

"Ed, I need to ask a favor."

"Sure, what d'ya need?"

"Well, Luther Cravens is upset. Says he's gonna sell the farm and move to Florida. I think he's just lonely and doesn't know what else to do."

"So what's the favor?"

"I wonder if you could talk to him. Just go out there and have a chat with him, see what's really eatin' him. I don't really think he wants to leave the community, he's just upset and needs a friend. Think you could do that?"

"Sure, I'll have a talk with him."

The next morning, Ed drove out to Luther's farm and found him in the barn, loading furniture into a two-wheeled trailer.

"How ya doin', Luther?" Ed began. "Looks like you're movin'."

Luther stopped loading and sat down on a bale of straw. He wiped his forehead with a large bandana handkerchief.

"Yeah, I think it's time to move on. Been on this old farm all my life. Time to see somethin' new. I'm thinkin' of movin' to Florida. I got a brother-in-law and his wife down there near Sarasota. They said there was houses for sale near 'em. Might be good for me. Give me a new outlook on life."

"Well, Luther, we'd all hate to see you go," Ed said. He sat down on a bale of straw. "You can go to Florida and see new stuff if you want, and not have to move down there, y'know. What if you get there and find out you don't like it?"

"I guess that's a chance I'll have to take," Luther said. He looked up at Ed. "Life's full o' chances. I'm fifty-five years old. If I'm ever gonna see anything, now's the time to do it."

"Listen," Ed said, "if it's a question of lookin' after the farm, lots of us can do that. Why don't you just take a little vacation down to Florida, see your relatives, and come home the long way—maybe through the Carolinas. I hear they're real purty. And when you get back, you'll be all refreshed and ready to pick up where you left off."

Luther looked thoughtful a moment.

"You don't understand, Ed. There's nobody here for me. It's a nice town and all, but I don't have nothin' to keep me here. Nobody really needs me."

"Heck, that ain't so!" Ed said. "We need each other in this town— all of us. You're just as important as any one of us."

Luther got up and extended his hand. "Thanks for comin' out, Ed, but I think I'll be leavin' pretty soon."

They shook hands, and Ed drove back into town.

That evening, as he and John and Myron sat in the hardware store, Ed told about the conversation.

"No use in him goin' off like that," Myron said. "Wouldn't seem like Thornburg without a Cravens on that farm." The others nodded agreement.

"Maybe I should go out there and have a talk with him," John said. "I think he's just lonely. Y'can't blame him, losin' his family and all. Must be a purty dreary existence."

When John got home he talked with Leona about Luther. The twins were present, too, but soon went up to their room.

"Listen," Junior said, "here's our chance to pull the best one yet. He's gonna load that trailer full of stuff, ready to move to Florida. We gotta talk to Butch, maybe get a couple other guys in on it." Then he outlined his plan, while James grinned and agreed.

Before they went to bed, the twins announced that they were going to Mike Mendenhall's house for a campout the following night.

"He invited us to sleep over in his tent in the backyard," Junior said. "We're takin' our sleeping bags. Can we have some cookies and stuff to eat?"

"Well, this is mighty sudden," Leona said. "You might have told us sooner. Do Michael's parents know about this?"

"Sure! I thought we told you about it last week. Heck, we been plannin' this for a month. We're even gonna cook our own breakfast outdoors."

"Well, put on some bug repellent," their mother said. "Those mosquitoes will eat you alive without it. What are you supposed to take for the breakfast?"

"I don't know, maybe some bacon. His mom's gonna make us some biscuit mix, and I guess we'll fry eggs."

The next afternoon the boys met Butch Collins and Skinny McIntyre, who lived next door to Butch, and went to Michael's house, where they dug out his tent and camping gear. Erecting the tent in his backyard under a white oak tree, they talked excitedly about the plan.

"Man, this'll be a blast," James said. "He'll have a conniption fit for sure."

At dusk, Mike's father came out to check on the boys before he went to bed.

"Everything OK? You guys got everything you need?"

"Fine, Dad," Mike answered from inside the tent. He shined his flashlight on his father's face. "See you in the morning."

"Night," his father said. "Sleep tight, and don't set anything on fire."

He went in the house and turned out the lights.

After giving the Mendenhalls enough time to get to sleep, the boys crept out of the tent and down the alley. They crossed Wood Street to Barton Road on the east edge of town, then turned north to County Road 50 S. Climbing the fence, they kept to the hedgerow on the east side of Luther's farm until they got to his barnyard. One by one they climbed the fence and tiptoed to the barn and went inside. Mike turned on his Boy Scout flashlight, partly covering it with his fingers. There sat Luther's two-wheeled trailer, loaded high with household belongings and covered with a tarpaulin tied on the four corners with rope. Mike put the flashlight on a post, and the boys went to work.

As quietly as they could, they untied the rope and removed the tarpaulin. Then, piece by piece, they handed the things from the trailer up into the haymow. The heavier pieces they tied to the hay lift and pulled them up on the block and tackle, swinging them over to the mow. After an hour or more, every piece of Luther's belongings lay in the haymow.

Now they started on the trailer. They found Luther's tools in a cluttered corner of the barn he called his shop. Bolt by bolt they took the trailer apart, hauling the sideboards and tailgate up to the mow, then the wheels, and finally the chassis, hoisted by the block and tackle. Working only by the glow of the flashlight took more time than they had calculated.

It was now after midnight. Covered with sweat and very thirsty, they sat a few minutes to rest.

"Why didn't we bring somethin' to drink?" James said. "We were really dumb."

"There's a pump in the barnyard," Junior said, "but it'd prob'ly make too much noise."

He looked out the small window in the gable of the barn toward the house. The house was dark.

"He must be sleepin' like a baby," he said. "You could go get us a drink of water, James."

"Why don't you go yourself?"

"You're the one that mentioned it."

They finally decided to pass on the idea and just get on with their work.

"This won't take long," Skinny said. "Heck, I done this kind of stuff a lot."

They began with the trailer chassis, putting on the wheels first, then the sideboards and tailgate. Then the furniture went in, as near as they could remember its order. Smaller items filled the spaces around it. By the time they had the tarpaulin tied on the corners, they were exhausted and wringing wet with sweat. But they were elated at their success. They climbed down the ladder, laughing at the prospect of Luther Cravens looking up at his trailer in the haymow and wondering how it got there.

Butch, having tied the final knot on the rope, was the last to start down. The twins had got halfway to the fence, with Skinny and Mike close on their heels, when a shotgun blast tore through the darkness behind them. Buckshot rattled in the trees above them. Running like deer for the fence, they vaulted over and sped along the opposite side of the hedgerow for home.

When Butch heard the shot, he froze on the ladder, hardly daring to breathe. He heard the retreating feet of his buddies, then the heavier footsteps of Luther Cravens entering the barn. Luther's flashlight searched the ground floor of the barn.

Butch heard him mutter aloud, "Why, them rascals have stole my trailer!" He looked out the barn door. "But where–?"

The gate to the road was closed, and weeds grew in front of it. Obviously, it had not been opened.

Perplexed, Luther turned back inside and threw the beam of his flashlight up into the mow. It fell squarely on Butch Collins, clinging to the ladder. The boy was shaking with fear; cold sweat ran down his face.

"You, there!" Luther shouted. "You better just come on down. I got ya dead to rights."

He kept the light on Butch until the boy got to the barn floor.

"You set down there," he commanded, indicating a bale of straw with his shotgun. He turned the light into the mow again. The loaded trailer stood out in the gloom like a weird apparition. Luther could hardly believe his eyes. He stared at the trailer as though it belonged to someone else.

"How in the hell did you do that?"

Butch sat grimly with his lips pressed firmly together, determined not to give his friends away. "I—just did it, that's all. I didn't mean nothin' harmful by it, it was just a joke."

"That ain't no joke," Luther said. "That's malicious. It'll take me a couple o' days to bring that down. You didn't do that alone! You had help, didn't ya? I heard someone runnin' for the fence. Who was it?"

Butch started to cry, and once he started, he couldn't stop. In his exhaustion and thirst, he sobbed and wiped his face with his grimy hands until it was muddy. But he refused to give the names of his friends. He was determined to take the blame alone. If he was ever to have friends again, he didn't dare rat them out. Luther set his shotgun against a stall and sat down on a bale beside the boy.

"Now cryin' ain't gonna get that trailer down, boy," he said. "You tell me who helped you do this, and we'll round 'em up and get that thing unloaded and back down here. And we'll just forget it ever happened."

"I ain't tellin' nothin'," Butch said through his tears. "You can beat me if you want to, but I ain't tellin' nothin'."

"Beating isn't gonna get that trailer down," Luther said, softening. "I don't aim to do you any harm. But I can't get it down by myself, and I was fixin' to leave town tomorrow."

He thought a minute, then said, "What's your name, Son?"

"Butch Collins."

"Where d'ya live?"

"Out on the anglin' road—last house." He wiped his face with the tail of his shirt. "I live with my sister and her husband."

"What their name?"

"Look, I don't wanna bring them into this. They didn't have nothin' to do with it. It was all my idea, and I'll take the blame for it. If you won't turn me in, I'll help you get the trailer down, and I'll do anything else you want if you'll just let me go. But I'm too tired to do it right now."

He turned his tear-streaked face to Luther, who studied him closely with the flashlight.

"Johnson," Luther said. "I know him now. Works at the elevator. He your sister's husband?"

Butch nodded. "But he didn't have nothin' to do with it."

"OK," Luther concluded, "I know where to find you. You go on home and rest. Come back tomorrow afternoon. You and I'll get that thing down, and then we'll have a talk, y' hear?"

"Yes Sir." Butch stood up on shaky legs and turned toward Luther. "Thanks for not beatin' me." He went out the barn door, climbed the gate, and trudged home.

Just after lunch the next day, Luther saw Butch coming to the side door of the farmhouse. He let the boy in.

"You had your lunch?"

"Yes, thanks. I come back to work on that trailer."

"Well, let's get at it then," Luther said. He handed Butch a pair of gloves. "You might need these."

They walked to the barn in silence. When they had climbed the ladder to the haymow, Luther directed Butch in untying the ropes and hauling off the tarpaulin, then he chuckled.

"I guess you'd know as much about this as I would, wouldn't you?"

"I guess so," Butch said. He glanced at Luther. "I can't believe you're bein' so nice to me. Most folks woulda beat me for doin' this, or turned me in to the marshal."

"That the way your family treats you?" Luther said.

"Randy beat me once when I broke his gun. It was the rear sight; I thought it lifted up, but it didn't. It just broke off. I was sorry, and I said so, but he beat me anyway."

"Well, that ain't nothin' to beat a boy over," Luther said, pulling off the tarp. "Beating never solved anything."

He lifted out a few pieces of furniture, then, with a distant gaze he said, "I beat my boy once, and now I wish I hadn't done it." His chin trembled, and his voice broke. He turned his back to Butch and pulled at something that wouldn't budge.

Butch had a sizeable pile of goods on his side of the trailer when Luther continued.

"My boy was lost in the war. Only nineteen. Died in Germany. He's buried over there somewhere. My wife and I always thought we'd go see the place, but she died of cancer before we could get there."

He looked at Butch, with the afternoon sunlight streaming through the slats in the barn side, and said quietly, "Matter of fact, he looked a lot like you." Tears streamed from his eyes and down his face. "He was a good boy, and I miss him more than anyone could ever know." He took out his bandana and wiped his eyes.

Butch hung his head and was quiet and uncomfortable. Then he said, "I'm sorry."

In a minute Luther recovered and went on emptying the furniture from the trailer. Butch helped him tie the larger pieces onto the block and tackle and lower them to the barn floor, then he went down the ladder to untie them. Together they unbolted the trailer, took off the wheels, and let the chassis down.

When they had the trailer and its contents on the barn floor, they began to reassemble it. Luther stopped with a chair in his hands and looked at Butch.

"Y'know, it's nearly suppertime, and I ain't sure I'm gonna leave so soon anyway. No hurry is there?" he said, almost to himself. "Tell you what. Let's go up to the house and eat some supper. Your folks expectin' you for supper?"

"I don't reckon so," Butch said. "Marjorie—that's my sister—ain't home. She went to the city with a friend of hers, and Randy's at work 'til dark. I usually just get myself somethin' out of the ice box."

"Well, we'll just have supper here," Luther said. He put a hand on the boy's shoulder. "I guess you're just kind of a leftover boy, aren't you? Fendin' for yourself like that. You don't really have any more family than I do."

"I guess not," Butch admitted.

They walked up to the house. Luther told him of being born on the farm and growing up there as an only child, then inheriting it from his folks when they died. "No place like home," he said. They went inside.

Luther fried some pork chops and potatoes and opened a quart of applesauce. He poured milk for both of them, and they ate together at the kitchen table. Luther told Butch about his own childhood, about some of the stunts he had pulled, and they laughed together.

"Yessir," Luther said, "you remind me a lot of myself in those years."

In the weeks and months that followed, Butch came regularly to Luther's farm, helping out with the chores, learning to bring in the cows at milking time, learning to clean the equipment and shovel out the stalls. It was his first real job; he enjoyed having a little money in his pocket. He and Luther often talked about what it meant to grow up and take responsibility in a community like Thornburg, and they talked about what Butch would do after high school.

"I never thought about it before," Butch said. "Guess I always thought I'd just work at the elevator or somethin' like that."

"You got a better mind than that," Luther said. "You ought to go to college—Purdue, maybe—learn dairy farmin' or animal husbandry– somethin' like that. You're a natural."

"I am?"

"Sure you are! You make good grades, don't you?"

"Pretty fair, I guess."

"You care if I talk with your sister about it?"

"We don't have any money for college," Butch said.

"We'll worry about that later," Luther said.

Marjorie Johnson was at first incredulous, then suspicious, then silent. She looked at Butch as if he were a stranger. Her husband was not at home.

"You sure about this?" she asked Luther.

"Yep. I want him to go to college. My own boy never got to. This is my chance to see the farm go on after me. Butch and I have become pretty close friends these past few months."

"Well, I don't care," Marjorie said, "long as it don't cost us nothin'."

She looked at Butch. "You sure you wanna do this?"

"I sure would like to," he answered.

So the decision was made. Butch planned to enter Purdue University in the fall after graduation from high school. In the intervening months, he came to think of Luther as a surrogate father, which pleased Luther more than he could say. He asked Butch if he would mind being called Frank, since it seemed a natural derivation of Francis. Butch said it would be OK.

When the twins heard about it, they looked confused. Junior said, "You ain't gonna be Butch no more?"

"You can call me Butch if you want to, but Luther wants to call me Frank. I kinda like it."

"Well, me and James don't really care, I guess. You'll still be our buddy, won't you?"

"Sure," he said.

Gradually, the town came to call him "Luther's boy, Frank." By spring the name seemed natural to his friends as well as to himself. His teachers stopped calling him Francis and accepted the shorter name.

Knowing that he was going to college had a salutary effect on the boy. His grades during his last year in high school were the best he had ever made. He and the Abbot twins were still friends, but they had no time for pranks. Senior year activities occupied them and seemed to mature their outlook. The three were becoming serious students, a fact which did not go unnoticed by their parents and teachers.

On a warm April afternoon, as Frank and Luther were working on a disk, Luther asked him how he would feel about being adopted as his son.

"My Gosh!" was all the boy could say. "You mean it?" He was obviously thrilled at the prospect.

"I've never had a dad."

"It'd mean the world to me," Luther said.

"It's OK with me," Frank said. "My gosh!"

So on the following Monday, Luther and Frank went to the courthouse in the county seat with Arlen Klein, the town's attorney, and Luther adopted the boy as his son. The Abbot twins were invited, along with their parents as witnesses. After the papers were signed, they all celebrated the occasion with dinner at a nice restaurant. Luther paid the bill.

At the high school graduation ceremony that year, the Abbott twins and Frank Cravens threw their caps in the air together with thirty-four other graduates. They had made it through the trauma of the teen years and looked forward to a future they knew little about. But they were ecstatic.

In the fall, a proud and happy Luther Cravens took his son to Purdue University for enrollment in the School of Agriculture. He never again talked of moving to Florida, and into his old age he and Frank ran the farm together.

Frank married Gloria Martindale from Mooresville, who had also been in the agriculture program. They shared the large Cravens farmhouse, bringing three children into Luther's life. He was a wonderful father, father-in-law, and grandfather. And every Christmas, lights from the decorated farmhouse illuminated the northern edge of Thornburg, Indiana.

The Windfall

On the morning of his twenty-ninth birthday, Doyle Case awoke to bright sunlight streaming in through his window. He got out of bed, put on his robe, and came downstairs barefooted to find his wife Beverly frying bacon and eggs. Their two children, Rachel, six, and Ethan, nearly eight, sat happily at their places, already halfway through bowls of Cheerios. Doyle kissed his wife on one cheek.

"Well, I made it!" he proclaimed. "I am now twenty-nine, the perfect age."

"What makes twenty-nine the perfect age?" asked Beverly. "When I turned twenty-nine last fall, I noticed my first gray hairs."

"Well, I don't have any gray hairs," Doyle said, "although I notice they're getting thinner up there. Oh, well! That doesn't matter. It's the perfect age anyway. It's the age I used to dream of being when I was in high school: still young, but mature enough to be taken seriously."

"Have you not felt that people take you seriously?" Beverly pursued. "I've taken you seriously since you asked me to marry you. You *were* serious about that, weren't you?"

"Never more so," he said, and kissed her other cheek. "But today is special. I can feel it. Today I'm . . ."

"A pharmacist," she said. "Having a birthday hasn't changed that, has it?"

"A significant person," he said, to finish his sentence. "I'm a—a mover and shaker in this town. I'm a person to be reckoned with."

"You're a person whose breakfast is getting cold."

"Daddy, sit down now," Rachel said. "Eat your eggs!"

"OK, gang, I'll eat my breakfast, and then I'll be significant later." He and Beverly held hands with the children and said their table grace together.

Beverly waited until Doyle had nearly finished with his breakfast before she brought in his birthday card and present. "From all of us," she said, and she led the kids in singing "Happy Birthday."

"Open the card first," Ethan said excitedly. "We made it! Rachel and I made it for you."

Doyle opened the envelope on which Beverly had written his name, under which each child had printed "Daddy." The card was decorated with pigs, a chicken, and a building with smoke coming out of the chimney and an Rx on one corner. Part of the phrase "Happy Birthday" had been successfully printed on the opposite side, but the crayon had run out of room. The children had signed their names.

Doyle was pleased and thanked them for "such a beautiful birthday card!" and promised to put it in a prominent place where he could look at it often. Then he opened the package which Beverly had laid at his place. It was covered in red, white, and blue striped paper tied with a silver ribbon. It seemed amazingly lightweight for a shirt box.

"Well, at least I know it isn't that set of socket wrenches I've been wanting," Doyle said. "Maybe it's a hundred dollar bill. They don't weigh much."

"Open it, open it!" cried Ethan and Rachel together, so Doyle pulled on the bow and untied the ribbon.

"You don't have to save the paper, Honey," Beverly said. "Just give it a rip."

When the lid was finally lifted, Doyle found only a card inside that read,

"A pair of goats has been given to the Sambaco family of The Congo in your name. These animals will provide milk and cheese for the family, and later a herd of goats for meat. Thank you for your compassion and generosity!"

The card was signed by a representative of their church's denominational mission program, and an explanatory brochure was included.

Doyle had a quizzical look, then a happy look. Finally he said, "Wow! That is so neat! You mean, this Sambaco family has a pair of goats that we sent them?"

"In honor of your birthday," his wife said.

"Look at this! There's a picture of the goats with the family. My gosh! They must have ten children! I hope goats give a lot of milk."

"They'll have kids," Beverly said, "and some of them will be females. In time, the family will have lots of milk, I expect."

"And butter and cheese," Ethan added. "And more little goats."

"That's right," Doyle said. He thought a moment, then added, "Do they know who sent the goats? I mean, do they have our name and address?"

"All that information is in the hands of the mission station in The Congo. I expect we'll hear something from them."

"That's really something! Friends in The Congo. I wish we could go over there and see them."

"We could see the goats, too," Rachel offered.

"Well, anyway, they'll have a better life now," Beverly said, "and all because your Daddy had a birthday."

"Thanks, Hon, that was a wonderful thing to do!" said Doyle. "I'm going up and get dressed, and then I think I'll take a walk in honor of my birthday. Thank Heaven for birthdays that come on a Saturday!"

Beverly was in the den, and the children were watching cartoons on TV, when Doyle stepped out of his front door into the sunshine of a May morning. It was perfect weather for a walk. He turned north and walked briskly up Clarion Street to Jefferson, then turned right and walked over to Main, where he got a drink at the fountain. He was feeling wonderful and decided to make a real hike of it. He walked north on Main past a row of stores that over the years had replaced a hotel, a livery stable, and a tavern. He passed their church, the school, and Devington Circle, the newest houses in town. At County Road 50 S he turned left and walked past the elevator, intending to cross the railroad and breathe some country air.

He had only just crossed the track when he noticed something shiny in the weeds beside the road. He looked at it more closely. It was an aluminum briefcase lying carelessly against a fence. He went over and picked it up, looking for identification, but there was none. He looked around to see if he could account for its presence—someone coming back for it, maybe. But no one was in sight. He carried the case along with him, wondering what he should do with it. It had not occurred to him to open it, because he felt that it was not his business. But how was he to find the owner unless he did?

At length, he turned around and went back the way he had come, south on Dark Street past Bennett's Park, then down Pike to Walnut. He wondered if anyone saw him carrying the briefcase; it was not his custom. When he got home, he found Beverly still in the den, paying bills. He set the briefcase on the table and said quietly, "Look what I found."

She looked up. "Where did you find it?"

"Out in the country, by the railroad. It doesn't have a tag on it or anything. I don't know whose it is."

"Well, is it locked? Can you open it? Maybe there's some identification inside."

He tried the thumb latches, but they didn't budge. "Nope, it's locked," he said.

"Well, I've got a bunch of keys from luggage and stuff," Beverly said. "Maybe one of them would open it."

"I don't think we ought to fool with it," Doyle said. "It isn't ours."

"But how will we ever know whose it is unless we open it?"

"Maybe I could get it open with a paper clip," Doyle ventured.

"Let's try the keys first," she said, and dug in the desk drawer until she produced a small box of keys.

"Where'd you get these?"

"I save them so they won't get lost," she answered. "Suitcase keys, the key to our lockbox, keys to little padlocks, stuff like that. Here, try this one."

He tried it, but it didn't fit. One by one they tried the keys in the box until one finally opened one of the latches. It didn't seem to work on the other latch, but Doyle fiddled with it until it yielded to his persistence. He opened the lid and gasped. Beverly got up and stared with him at the contents of the briefcase. It was filled with more money than they had ever seen!

Neither of them spoke. Doyle closed the door to the den and came slowly back. Beverly gingerly touched the money to assure herself that it was real, then she said in a whisper, "What have you got yourself into?" She looked at her husband.

"I don't know," Doyle said in a small voice. He picked up a package of bills and riffled through them. They were all hundred-dollar bills, obviously genuine, not new but used. They had rubber bands around them and did not look like they had come from a bank. There seemed to be nothing to identify the owner. Doyle closed the lid and locked it.

They looked soberly at each other. Doyle set the briefcase on the floor between the desk and the filing cabinet. Then he put his hands on his wife's shoulders, and looking directly into her eyes he said, "We'll have to think carefully about this. And we have to keep it to ourselves. You understand? We have to have time to think this out and do the right thing."

"Well, of course we'll do the right thing," Beverly said. "We'll turn it in to the marshal."

"Not just yet," Doyle said. "See, if Ted knows we have it, then he has to put that in a report, and then it's public knowledge. What if it's drug money? Some drug dealer reads in the newspaper that it's been found, and it's only a matter of time before he traces it to us. They'll be on the lookout for it anyway. They'll remember where they threw it out, probably escaping from the police."

"We don't know that it's drug money," she said.

"What else could it be?" he said. "Banks don't transport money that way."

"Couldn't we just tell Ted to keep our names out of it?" she asked.

"I don't think he can legally do that," Doyle replied. "It's the law that anyone involved in a crime has to be reported."

"But we're not involved in a crime!" Beverly insisted. "You just found this briefcase. You didn't know what was in it."

"That doesn't make any difference, we'll be involved just the same."

They were quiet a moment, and Beverly sat down again in her chair. Doyle leaned against the filing cabinet. The sound of cartoons from the living room filled the silence.

At last Beverly said, "Well, I'm not comfortable with it here in the house. I wish you'd take it to the bank and put it in a safety deposit box. That'd give us time to think."

"The bank's closed on Saturday," he said dryly.

"Well, it can't sit there," she said. "The kids will ask about it, and I'm not going to lie to them."

"I'll put it in my closet upstairs," Doyle said.

He put the briefcase in a shopping bag from Beverly's collection in the den closet, then went upstairs to the bedroom, where he secreted the case behind a stack of sweaters on the top shelf of his closet. When he came down again he was not the carefree birthday boy he had been. He looked worried and was quiet. He and Beverly checked on the children, then sat in the kitchen to talk.

They tried to think through every scenario that was likely to occur: strange cars patrolling the town looking for the briefcase, questions asked around town of the grocer, the banker, the barber, maybe even door to door. Would a stranger know a guilty face if he saw one? Would Ted Bates ask if anyone had found the money? What would they tell him?

"Maybe we could put an anonymous notice in the paper . . ." Doyle began, and then quickly dismissed the idea. Same problem: it would eventually be traced to them.

"We could just leave it at the marshal's office some night," Beverly suggested, "with a note that it had been found by the railroad."

"And how do we know someone else wouldn't pick it up before the marshal found it?" Doyle said. "And he'd be sure to ask questions around town until he finally figured out it was us."

"Did anyone see you carrying it home?"

"I don't think so. I didn't see anyone."

She was quiet a long time before she said, "Well, we need to think more on it. Let's not talk it to death until we have a good idea what to do with it."

"OK," he said, and they dropped the subject.

He went outside to cut the grass, and Beverly did her usual Saturday chores. Then she baked a rhubarb pie. But the money occupied their minds constantly.

After supper dishes were done, the family retired to the living room and listened to "The Grand Old Opry." Then it was the children's bedtime. Ethan was unusually quiet through the evening. When his mother tucked him in bed he asked, "Is Daddy OK, Mommy? He doesn't seem happy with his birthday anymore."

"Daddy's fine, Honey," Beverly assured him. "He's just tired and has a lot on his mind. Now you sleep tight!" And she kissed him goodnight and pulled the cover up to his chin.

He pulled it down partway and said, "Would you leave my bear lamp on?"

"OK, now go to sleep." She closed his bedroom door.

Rachel was already asleep when she looked in on her again, so she left her night light on and closed her door. She went quietly downstairs, where she found Ted in the den. She joined him there, rubbing his shoulders a while. He was making a list of all the possibilities for dealing with the money.

At last he looked up and said, "How about if I talk with our pastor? He keeps confidences well. I know, I've talked with him about other things. I'm sure he's trustworthy."

Beverly sighed and said, "That might be a good idea. But you'd have to swear him to secrecy before you ever told him."

"I just thought maybe he'd have an idea what to do."

"Maybe. I can't think of anything else to do," she answered.

After the Sunday morning service, Doyle went to Pastor Harold Markham's office as he was hanging up his robe. Markham was a man in his late forties with enough experience to listen and reflect without giving advice. He had been the pastor of the church for seven years, and the congregation loved and trusted him.

"May I have a minute of your time, Pastor?" Doyle asked.

"Why sure, Doyle. Come in." Markham closed the door and offered Doyle a chair. "What can I do for you?"

"Well, I need to talk to you," Doyle said, still standing. "Not now, there isn't time. But maybe later this afternoon, if you aren't too busy."

"How about three o'clock?" the pastor suggested.

"That'd be fine," Doyle said. "It's something that's been on my mind, and I need some guidance. I think you might be the one to help me."

"I'll sure do my best," Markham said. "Three o'clock, then?"

"See you at three," Doyle said, and left the office.

The Case family ate their usual Sunday dinner: chuck roast with potatoes, carrots, and onions around it, the aroma of which was marvelous when they came in from church. Rhubarb was Doyle's favorite pie; it lifted his heaviness for a while as he savored its tart sweetness.

While Beverly cleared the table, Doyle read the Sunday paper, answered a phone call from one of his customers at the drug store, reassured her that the pills the doctor had prescribed would not affect her memory, and fell asleep in his Lazy Boy for ten minutes. About a quarter to three he walked up to the church and met Pastor Markham in his office.

He told the story of finding the briefcase and their consternation regarding its contents. "We want to do the right thing, but everything we think of has drawbacks," he said.

"This is one of the most unusual problems I've ever heard of," Markham said. "And you're probably right; it's probably drug money."

"But why wouldn't they come back for it?" Doyle wondered.

"Too much risk, I suppose," Markham said. "Or maybe they're in jail."

Then he smiled and said, "It's really every man's dream, isn't it? Finding a lot of money with no way to trace the owner. But I see your dilemma. You want to do the right thing, but it's hard to know just what that is."

"If there was some way to get it to the proper authorities without anyone knowing who brought it . . . ." Doyle thought a moment, and then he asked, "What would the authorities do with it, anyway?"

"I'm not sure," the pastor said. "I think it would go into a general fund of some kind, maybe for police pensions or something. I could ask some law enforcement people I know."

"No, I'm afraid that would raise more questions," Doyle said. "I hate to just turn it over to the authorities. You read so much about unscrupulous cops and judges and lawyers, I'm afraid it would never be heard of again."

"Well, I really don't have the answer," Markham said, "but you need to do what you believe God would have you to do. Take your time and think about it, pray about it. You'll know eventually what to do."

"I sure hope so," Doyle said.

"And if you'd like to talk again, I'm always here."

"I sure thank you, Pastor." He shook Markham's hand and left for home.

Beverly and the children were in the backyard when he returned, and he went out to join them. His wife looked at him inquiringly. He smiled and said, "It'll be OK," and pushed Rachel in her swing.

That night, after the kids were asleep, Doyle took the briefcase from the top shelf in the closet and opened it on the bed. Beverly came in as he was counting out hundred dollar bills and exclaimed, "What on earth are you doing!"

"I just wondered how much is here."

"That isn't going to help us figure out what to do with it," she said. "It'll only make it harder to let go of."

"I guess I gotta admit I've thought about all the things we could do with it. It sure would make our lives a lot easier. It's a real windfall."

"That kind of thinking will get us into trouble," his wife said. "We start looking prosperous, and the whole town'll wonder what we've been doing on the side. We have to get rid of it."

"I know you're right," he said. "As soon as I can figure out the right thing to do with it. I just wanted to know how much we're talking about."

The money was wrapped in bundles of fifty, each bundle worth $5,000. There were fifty bundles neatly stacked, a total of $250,000. Doyle stared at the money in the briefcase. Beverly leaned over and closed the lid.

"That's enough wishing," she said. "If we don't find a way to get rid of it soon, it's going to ruin us. We'll be sneaking it out to the grocery and the department store and who knows where else, and pretty soon it'll be known that we have it. *And it isn't ours,*" she emphasized, looking directly at him.

Doyle locked the case and put it back on the shelf. "You're right," he said. "But we sure could use it—maybe get it into a trust fund for the kids' education. Have you thought of that?"

"I haven't let myself dwell on it," she answered, "because I know how I am. If I think about it too much, it'll begin to work on me, and then I'll be trying to find some way to keep it. Let's go downstairs."

They immersed themselves in the Sunday paper again, then listened to the radio a while. Just after ten o' clock they turned out the lights and went back upstairs to bed.

Doyle slept fitfully and got up two or three times to go to the bathroom or get a drink of water. About three o'clock he woke Beverly and said, "I think I've got it."

"What?" she asked in a sleepy voice.

"Those goats," he began.

"What about them?"

"That's where we'll send the money—to The Congo. What do you think?"

"Can we talk about it in the morning?"

"OK," he said, and turned over and went to sleep.

On Monday morning Doyle called Shirley Cartwright, his assistant at the drugstore, and asked her to cover for him until he "took care of some business." Then he called Pastor Markham and asked to come see him.

"I realize it's your day off, Pastor, but I think we've figured out the answer."

"Good for you," Markham said. "I can meet you in my office in about thirty minutes."

In Markham's office, Doyle outlined the plan he and Beverly had agreed to. Pastor Markham thought a few moments before he answered.

"So you're going to launder the money by sending it to The Congo."

"I kinda thought of it as baptizing it," Doyle said.

Markham smiled. "Well, that's one way of looking at it, I guess. I have to tell you, though, that I made some inquiries last night. I have a good friend in law enforcement in another town. He said that unless someone is apprehended for a crime and it can be shown that the money is evidence, it's really a case of finders-keepers. But I do think your concern is well founded. Whoever threw that money out a car window or whatever surely wants it back. But I don't think there have been any strangers out along the track this weekend. Clara Lyons would certainly have called me by now if there had been. She watches out her kitchen window over there on Devington Circle for anything new that comes by and reports to me. I don't know what she thinks I should do about it, but I get the news just the same."

"Well, Pastor, if you think it's all right, I'd like to go ahead with our plan."

"I think it's a good plan, Doyle," Markham said. "It ought to baptize that money just fine."

So at the Tuesday night Church Council meeting, Pastor Markham outlined a proposal to begin a mission program in The Congo.

"Our church already has work going on there, and the need is great. I think we should make a contribution to it. I'm proposing that we take up a special offering every fourth Sunday of the month for the people of The Congo."

After some questions and assurance that it wouldn't cut into the budget, the council agreed that a special offering wouldn't hurt anything. So the motion was made and passed, and the council went on to other business.

On Sunday morning Pastor Markham announced the special offering for the following Sunday. He said that special offering envelopes would be placed in the pews, and folks could give to The Congo in those envelopes—"over and above the regular offerings," he was quick to point out.

During the announcements the following Sunday morning, Pastor Markham asked that everyone put an offering in the special envelope, "even if it's only a penny. We need to participate in this thing together."

So when the offering plates were passed, dozens of special offering envelopes went into them. When the pastor put the plates on the altar, the pile of envelopes bound for The Congo was clearly visible, mixed in with the regular offerings.

The next morning Markham called Doyle. "You ready for this? Twenty-seven hundred and sixty dollars, and twenty-seven cents!"

Doyle laughed delightedly and said, "So someone really did put in a penny!"

"Two pennies, actually," Markham said. "I think the congregation will be stunned when they see how much they gave. Thanks for the idea, Doyle. It's going great!"

Every fourth Sunday of the month thereafter, Doyle slipped the pastor a handful of hundred-dollar bills, and every special offering was wonderful. Not only did Doyle's money create a substantial contribution to the Congo mission, it inspired giving among the members of the congregation. Each month the amount increased, well beyond Doyle's gift. The idea was catching on.

On the first Sunday in September, Pastor Markham read a letter to the congregation from the Congo mission.

To our dear Friends in Thornburg, Indiana:

We hardly know how to thank you for your generous outpouring of love for our mission here! This summer we have been able to buy a herd of goats for every family in our parish, plus pigs and chickens.

Our people are better fed than they have ever been. Some of the money we have used in our mission hospital, and many lives have been saved because of your kindness. Thank you for responding so faithfully to the Holy Spirit's leading! We remember you every Sunday in prayer. God bless you all!

It was signed by the leader of the mission.

The congregation applauded. Paul Forester asked the pastor to respond to the letter, saying how much this mission had meant to the church in Thornburg.

"I notice that our overall giving has increased since we began this special offering," he said. "I think we should just keep it up."

Several "Amens" were heard from the pews. Pastor Markham promised that it would become part of his annual recommendation to the church.

During the next few years other projects were initiated and funded. The church thrived. No one ever knew about the "seed money," but they gave generously, astonished at the amount they were able to raise.

It took eight years to dispose of all the money in the briefcase. Doyle never took it off his top shelf, fearful that opening a large deposit box at the bank might cause suspicion.

On the morning of his thirty-seventh birthday his wife presented him with a box neatly wrapped in gold paper and tied with a silver ribbon.

"Silver and gold have I none; but such as I have give I thee," she said, quoting St. Peter.

Doyle smiled and kissed her and opened the box. Inside was a beautiful brown leather briefcase with his initials on the clasp.

"For your out-of-town trips to the druggists' convention," she said.

"It's beautiful!" he responded. "Thanks, Hon!" He smelled the new leather and looked into all its compartments. Then he asked, "What did you do with the other one?"

"I took it with me on that last trip to Ft. Wayne and threw it in a dumpster," she said.

They both laughed and hugged each other, and Doyle said, "That has to be the greatest adventure we've ever had!"

"And to think," she said, "it all started with a pair of goats!"

Hattie

Hattie Frances Cooper was the only person of African descent in Thornburg. She had come from Louisiana in the early 1930s with her mother to escape the poverty of the Great Depression in the South. Her father had died of influenza in 1918. Her mother's sister lived in the last house on the west edge of Thornburg, across a field at the end of Walnut Street. It had been a farmhouse in the nineteenth century where the aunt was a maid and nanny. It was left to her at the owner's death. Hattie and her mother moved in. The aunt died in 1936, Hattie's mother in 1939, and Hattie was left alone at 51 years old to fend for herself.

A tall, thin woman, she wore cotton print dresses that hung from her bony shoulders to mid-calf, never tied at the waist, and often supplemented by a gray knit sweater. The clothes had belonged to her mother and aunt. None of them really fit her, none of them matched, but it didn't seem to matter to her. She walked across her field to town every day, in good weather and bad, sometimes with a large black umbrella she called a "parasol." A brown canvas bag hung from her shoulder by a heavy strap, carrying her "p'ticulars." Everyone knew her simply as Hattie.

How she made a living was a mystery. She had few visible means of support, yet she never begged. Sometimes she worked in homes, cleaning or cooking. Most times she walked the streets or, in summer, worked in her garden. Her presence in times of emergency was legendary, but never explained. Once she stopped at a house on a hunch to find a young mother in labor, her husband away, and the baby too near delivery for Dr. Call to be found or an ambulance to be summoned. Within minutes of her arrival, Hattie had helped deliver the child, tied the umbilical cord, laid the baby on the mother's belly, and cleaned up the afterbirth before calling the doctor.

What she carried in her bag was the greatest mystery of all. The things she drew from it in moments of necessity seemed foreordained: bandages, pencils, hard candy that stopped a child's tears, a screwdriver that saved Marty Hutchins's hanging plant from certain demise. A coach's whistle she gave to a high school girl one afternoon proved its worth at two o'clock in the morning, when a dark figure climbed a trellis outside the girl's bedroom window. Hearing something strange, she went to the window and saw a man reaching for her window sash. She snatched the whistle from her dresser and blew it loudly. The man dropped to the ground and ran. The girl's father got to her bedroom in time to see the intruder escaping down the alley.

A button Hattie brought forth from her bag one afternoon was the exact match for a missing one on Della Paul's coat. A key she had found was one Ed Porter had lost on his way to make a new one for the town's attorney, Arlen Klein. Somehow she seemed to know where it belonged. She went to the law office and laid it on Arlen's desk without a word. He stared at it.

"Where'd you find that?"

"In the gutter, Mista Klein. I thought you might need it."

"How'd you know it was mine?"

"I don't know, Mista Klein, it just seemed right."

Herbs that Hattie produced from her bag often soothed headaches or inflamed joints. She had ancient remedies from the South that seemed strange and unlikely to Hoosiers, but they often cured ills that other medicines did not. She gathered weeds from the roadsides and along Bode's Creek, hanging them to dry in her kitchen or back porch. Some she made into "potions" she mixed and kept in an odd assortment of bottles. Some she reduced to powder, grinding them in a wooden bowl with the back of a wooden spoon. She had her believers as well as her detractors; some swore by her remedies and others scoffed or ignored her. People often tried to pay her for her remedies, but she wouldn't take any money.

"All you has to do is want it," she would say.

Every summer she raised a garden, canning tomatoes and corn, drying onions and what she called "leather breeches beans" for the rest of the year. She kept a root cellar in which her potatoes, beets, carrots, and turnips lasted through the winter.

A hand-woven straw hat protected her head in summer, tied under her chin by a cord she had braided from fibers of milkweed stalks. Around her neck, morning and night, she wore a cross carved from a branch of the dogwood tree. She said her great uncle had made it for her when she was born, and she would never be without it, that it was her protection from evil.

Often she carried a walking stick, more as a talisman than as support. At its upper end she had carved odd figures: a sun and moon, a spiral that ran three times around the stick, a cross, and something like runes that she never explained.

"They's just my own language," she would say.

Sometimes, for no apparent reason, she would hold the stick in front of her with both hands, close her eyes, and mumble inaudible things. To children she was both friend and mystery; to adults she was simply an odd part of the scenery. She posed no threat to the community, so she was allowed to be strange and inexplicable.

One hot August day, Hattie waded in Bode's Creek, singing songs she had learned in her childhood. A small boy trying to cross the creek on a log slipped and fell in, striking his head on a rock. Hattie was instantly by his side, pulled him from the water, and carried him up the creek bank. Then she ran with the child through the streets of town to Dr. Call's office on Maple Street. She sat with the boy while Dr. Call examined him and called his parents.

The anxious mother arrived in less than a minute, breathing hard. Hattie was holding the boy and rocking him gently.

"He's gonna be all right," she assured the mother.

"He has a mild concussion," the doctor said. "Just keep him quiet for the next twenty-four hours, and I think he'll be fine."

The mother and Hattie took turns carrying the boy home, where he lay in bed the rest of the afternoon. Hattie sat with the boy and his mother, singing softly, stroking his head, until he regained consciousness in the early evening. His mother had called her husband at work. He came home early from the Sinclair Station.

"We don't know how to thank you, Hattie," he said. "You saved his life."

"Dat's all the thanks I need," she said, and left quietly.

Some folks in town said she was "in league with the devil," that the things she did were voodoo and no Christian should go near her. Others saw in her the embodiment of a free soul, the model of a true Christian, for she gave of herself for others. She asked nothing in return for the help she rendered. No one ever heard an unkind word from her, no one ever found her mean-spirited. She seemed continually happy. She taught her songs to the children who followed her to the fields in summer, so long as their parents would let them. In winter she wore four-buckle arctics and a heavy cloth coat that came to her ankles, exchanging the summer straw hat for a woolen scarf she had made. Weather had little effect on her.

Over time, some residents of the town came to trust her intuition or "voodoo" or whatever folks chose to call it. Her hunches were usually correct, sometimes eerily so. She once warned the marshal that an escaped convict she had heard about would come through Thornburg the next day. Not wanting to take any chances, Marshal Bates kept an eye out for strangers. About dusk he saw a man he did not recognize walking slowly along the sidewalk, looking into cars parked along the curb. Glancing around, the man opened a car door.

Ted came up behind him and said, "That your car?"

The man was startled and blurted out, "Of course it is!"

"May I see your license?" Ted asked.

The man bolted across the street and ran between the houses. Ted got in his car and followed him across town, running him to ground beyond the lumberyard. He was indeed an escaped convict, with a record in three states for armed robbery and car theft. The marshal transported him to the county jail. Then he looked up Hattie. She was sitting on her front porch.

"Jus' soakin' up the sweet night air," she told him.

Ted pulled up a rocking chair and sat down. "Hattie, how did you know an escaped convict would come to town today?"

"Marshal, I don't know nothin' fer sure, I just gets hunches. I don't know where dey come from."

"Well, Hattie, you probably saved Charlie Smith's car this evening. I apprehended a man about to steal it off Main Street. You were right: he had a record as long as my arm. Wanted in three states. He'd escaped from jail over in Ohio. We owe you a debt of thanks for warning us, however you knew it."

"Marshal, nobody owes me nothin'. De only one we owe is God himself. He's the one who guides us all. Trouble is, most folks don't listen."

"Well, I'll try to listen closer from now on," the marshal said. He stood to leave, extending his hand to Hattie. "Thanks for telling me your hunches!" He smiled and said, "Keep 'em comin'."

The spring of 1950 had seen a polio epidemic in Indiana, and people lived in fear of its coming to Thornburg. Dr. Call had exhorted everyone to wash their hands frequently, stay out of crowds, travel only if necessary, and get plenty of rest. He posted notices on the drugstore's front door, the bank, and Barclay's Restaurant.

"So far, there's no cure for it," he said. "We all have to take every precaution against it."

"What do *you* think about this polio epidemic, Hattie?" Mrs. Billings asked her one afternoon in June. She had just come from the drugstore where she had been discussing the epidemic with Doyle Case.

Hattie raised up from drinking at the town fountain and said, "We got to take action."

She leaned against the fountain and sprinkled cool water on her head, closing her eyes as if in a trance.

"And what kind of action do you recommend?" asked Mrs. Billings.

"We got to put a p'tective circle 'round de town," Hattie said. "It's de only way."

"And just what would that be?" Mrs. Billings pursued.

Hattie did not answer immediately, but with her eyes still closed she seemed to sway against the fountain as if she might fall. Mrs. Billings held her by the shoulders to steady her.

"Are you all right, Hattie?" she asked.

"You got to believe in it, first," Hattie said, ignoring the question. "It don't work if you don't believe."

"Well, suppose you tell me what it is first, and then I'll tell you if I believe in it."

Hattie straightened against the fountain and reached into her bag, withdrawing a fistful of weeds she had gathered in the field behind her house.

"Dis is the p'tection," she said. "We need to put it all around de town. Dat's what it needs. Den de polio won't come in here."

"Hattie, that's nothing but yarrow," Mrs. Billings said. "It's just a common weed. How on earth do you suppose it's going to stop polio?" She was the president of the Garden Club and prided herself on her knowledge of the local flora.

"Oh, Miz Billings, it's much more dan a weed. Folks all over de world know it cures lots of things. You gotta have faith." Her eyes were wide open as she looked into Mrs. Billings's face. "Do you have faith?"

"Oh, Hattie!" Mrs. Billings said in exasperation, "If you think it'll help, then go sprinkle it around town. It won't hurt anything." Then she added, "You're sure you're all right?"

"Jes fine, Miz Billings, thank you." And she walked slowly around the corner.

By the end of the week Hattie had gathered armloads of yarrow and piled them on her front porch. Then she told all the children she could find to come and take some to the edges of town and crumble the flower heads onto the ground. "Lay de stalks in groups of four, like de Chinese do," she instructed them. "Den walk ten steps and lay four more." The children trusted her completely; they began to distribute the yarrow around the town's perimeter.

Several mothers got wind of the scheme and sought out Hattie. She was searching along Bode's Creek for more yarrow when they found her.

"Hattie, what on earth are you doing with our children?" they demanded. "They're all over town with those weeds you collected, saying they're going to prevent polio! That's nonsense!"

All Hattie said was, "Wait and see."

As cases of polio were reported in other communities throughout the state, none were found in Thornburg. Throughout the summer the town waited in fear, but none of its citizens were touched by the plague. Folks began to look at Hattie differently, some in fear as though she had a supernatural power, others in amusement—as though yarrow could have anything to do with the town's health! Surely Dr. Call's precautions were the answer! Good hygiene was protecting them, nothing else. And yet they wondered.

"Do you think Hattie's yarrow has had anything to do with the town avoiding polio?" Beverly Case asked her husband.

Doyle sighed and shook his head. "I really don't know what to think. It's true that yarrow has been used for centuries for common ailments like colds, nosebleed, headache, and so on. But as far as preventing polio . . . ."

"Well, a lot of people in town are starting to believe Hattie's a miracle worker," Beverly said.

"I know, I know," Doyle answered. "Something's sure keeping it out of Thornburg, that's for sure! Makes you wonder, doesn't it?"

"Doyle," Beverly continued, "Do you think Hattie's OK? She's seemed stranger than usual lately. Preoccupied, I think."

"She always seems preoccupied to me," Doyle answered. "You think she's sick or something?"

"I don't know. She just doesn't seem quite like herself lately."

By the week before Thanksgiving, Hattie had attained a reputation as The Thornburg Angel, protecting the citizens against the plague of polio.

"Heck! I don't care what they call her," Myron Dunwiddie said, as he and Ed Porter discussed the disease-free summer and fall they'd enjoyed. "Maybe it's just good luck, or maybe she did have something to do with it. She's the only one who actually *did* anything about it."

"Did you hear her latest?" Ed said. "Now she's predicting a huge snowstorm for Thanksgiving. Four or five feet of it, she says."

"Hadn't heard that. Reckon you oughta buy more snow shovels?"

Ed chuckled and said, "I think I'll wait and see how much falls first. I don't want to be stuck with a store full of snow shovels when spring comes."

Hattie's prediction had pretty well circulated through the town when the first snow began to fall the day before Thanksgiving.

"Well, by gosh, she was right!" folks declared. They laughed at the coincidence and said it sure made the town look pretty.

But the snow did not stop on Thanksgiving Day; it continued through the night and all the next day, a blizzard the likes of which Thornburg had not seen in the lifetime of any of its residents. By

Saturday morning the cars parked along the streets were covered in snow. The state snow plows made a single lane down the middle of Main Street; the side streets were left to the feeble equipment of the town. The county highway department worked double shifts to clear the roads and rescue stranded motorists. Houses outside of town were inaccessible to mail delivery. Several families had finished the remnants of their Thanksgiving dinner and now opened canned goods for their meals. A few hardy souls slogged through the streets to carry groceries to older residents and check up on their neighbors.

It was more than a week before the town was operating on its usual schedule. Snow stood in heaps at the corners. Some cars still had not been dug out, but most folks went about their business. Melvia Markham asked her husband if anyone had thought to check on Hattie. He said he didn't know but would inquire. By evening, he had determined that no one had seen her since before Thanksgiving. He and Harry Corman, the Baptist minister, decided to make a trek out to her house.

They tramped through the unbroken snow across the field to the old farmhouse, panting for breath from lifting their legs over the drifts. They knocked on the door and called her name. No answer. Opening the door, they peeked inside. No Hattie. They walked through the rooms, calling her name, dodging bundles of dried herbs and leather breeches beans hanging from the transoms, from door handles and hooks on the walls. Braids of onions covered one wall of the kitchen. The pungent aroma made the house seem like a garden. The rooms were cold; the fire in the heating stove had gone out. The men went upstairs, their breath following them in clouds.

They found Hattie in the front bedroom, lying in bed with the covers pulled up to her chin. Around her lay fresh flowers: daisies, carnations, roses, violets. The men stood still and stared.

"Hattie?"

There was no response. Harold took her wrist and checked for a pulse. There was none.

They stood silent for a minute, then Harry Corman said, "She laid herself out for burial, didn't she?"

"But where did the flowers come from?" asked Harold. "These are spring flowers. There's no way a florist could have brought them! Not with all the snow!"

"I don't know," Harry said.

They stood a minute with their heads bowed, and Harry said a brief prayer for her soul. They left her and went back across the field to Clayton's Funeral Home. They told Melvin how they had found Hattie.

"What's remarkable about it is, she's surrounded by fresh flowers, the kind you don't find this time of year except at a florist. Do you know if any florist has come into town in the past week?"

"None that I know," Melvin replied. "I don't see how they could get here. Should I go get the body? Who's in charge of her?"

"I guess the town will have to pay for her funeral," Harold said. "The ministers will see to it that a service is held."

"Well, as soon as we can open the grave, you're welcome to hold it here," Melvin said. They agreed on Monday at two o'clock.

The heavy blanket of snow had protected the ground from a hard freeze. The cemetery workers were able to dig the grave in time for the Monday service. The town's only snowplow made a path to the cemetery and around the circle drive. Then a couple of men with shovels cleared a path to the grave.

Pastors announced the funeral in the churches on Sunday, and more than a hundred people came. The flowers that lay around Hattie on her bed now stood in vases at either end of her casket. Harold Markham and Harry Corman shared the service. Several folks braved the snow and mud to follow the hearse to the cemetery, where they laid Hattie to rest beside her mother and aunt, her flowers placed carefully on top of her grave.

As the committal ended and folks left to go back home, a boy of eight or nine left his mother's side and went to the grave. He pulled from his coat pocket a single stalk of yarrow he had kept since summer and, reaching across the flowers, stuck it in the soil over the place where Hattie's heart lay still.

"Goodbye, Hattie," he said. Then he whispered, "I love you," and went home with his family.

The Prettiest Girl in Town

Carla VanDyke lived in a two-story brick house on the northeast corner of Pike and Walnut Streets in Thornburg. The older of two daughters born to Walter and Evelyn VanDyke, she was by nearly total public acclamation known to be "the prettiest girl in town." Her Dutch ancestry almost guaranteed her long blond hair, china blue eyes, and fair complexion, dotted lightly about her nose and cheeks with freckles. As a high school junior, she was the heartthrob of at least two-dozen boys and the envy of nearly every girl in her class. And, even more remarkable, she was unspoiled.

Her sister, Gretchen, was four years younger and showed promise of being as pretty as Carla. Walter and Evelyn had worked hard at the job of parenting. The girls knew that good looks are simply gifts of God, not to be claimed as personal accomplishments, and certainly not to be strutted about town as allurements to boys or put-downs to other girls. Carla was quiet and studious, serious about school and church and community service. She made straight As in her junior year, and she was president of her church's youth fellowship. On Saturdays she worked as a candy striper at the hospital in the county seat eleven miles away. Occasionally she stayed with the Case children while Doyle and Beverly got a night out.

She was, in a word, perfect. Too perfect to suit some of the girls in town whose grades were not nearly as good as hers, who looked in their mirrors each morning with despair of ever attaining Carla's level of physical attraction. Oh, she dressed like the others: gray wool skirt that came to mid-calf, hose with bobby socks, saddle oxfords, a white blouse with a frilly panel in front and a pastel cardigan sweater. It was practically a uniform in the school, but on Carla it seemed somehow closer to perfection.

The boys wore corduroy trousers or jeans with cuffs turned up, sweaters or print shirts in winter and T-shirts in warmer weather with the sleeves turned up three or four times to expose their muscles. Dale Prentiss folded a pack of cigarettes into his sleeve when school hours were over. His long blond hair swept away from his forehead, catching the girls' attention. He drove his own car to school from his home on the south end of town, a red '49 Chevy convertible that simply drove the girls wild. He claimed that one ride in his car, especially at night, and any girl in town would be his.

Myra Logsdon was Carla's closest friend, mostly because she could see that beneath Carla's beauty was a wholesome and centered person who cared about people and intended to make her life count for something. Myra was pretty enough in her own way, but quite different from Carla. Her hair was straight and brown, her face simple and sweet, and she dressed nicely. But there was nothing vivacious about her, nothing that turned boys' heads as she passed on the street or in the halls at school. She was shy in groups and quiet in class, speaking only when called upon. She did not volunteer for committees, but if Carla asked her to help out on one, she would. She was a good student; her grades alone made her the envy of some other juniors.

The two often studied together. After Carla had her driver's license, they would drive to the county seat shopping. Myra's parents thought sixteen was too young for a girl to be driving alone. Carla was seventeen on January 3, so Myra was allowed to ride with her. Myra would not turn seventeen until March, and even then she was not permitted to take passengers. Her folks, Bud and Darlene Logsdon, were called old-fashioned by some. In that respect they were much like Carla's folks. The girls were guided by a clear sense of direction handed down from their parents. Neither of them questioned their parents' wisdom in matters of behavior or morals, in issues of school or community responsibility. Questions were dealt with openly and fairly, and the girls adhered to the values they had been taught.

The junior prom was, without doubt, the largest event in the life of a Thornburg student. The seniors had graduation, of course, and parties to celebrate it. But the junior prom was a rite of passage, a coming-out of those who would be leaders in the next year. The class officers worked hard to make each prom more spectacular than the previous year's, and their parents participated as if reliving their own high school days. A king and queen of the junior class were elected in the days preceding the prom. They reigned throughout the coming year as co-leaders of the senior activities.

So as the prom drew near, parents and students alike were busy making plans for decorating the gym, establishing a theme, and finding a band to play for the dance. Most of the boys were trying to get up enough courage to ask a girl to the prom, but none had asked Carla. It was generally accepted that Don Belson was her boyfriend, although they were not perpetually together the way most of the dating couples were. Don worked part-time at Spencer's Bakery, mixing dough for doughnuts, stocking flour, sugar, and yeast, and sometimes waiting on customers. He was a good-looking boy with a hank of dark hair and a muscular build. He played right guard on the basketball team and saw to his lessons faithfully. Part of his devotion to study came from his coach's insistence that the team keep up their grades, and part of it was his parents' vigilance over his activities.

Don and Carla were sometimes seen at the pizza parlor together, or walking hand in hand in the park in the late afternoon. His friends teased him about Carla, but he grinned and said that jealousy was a terrible thing and they should find someone to walk with themselves. Sometimes Don came to Carla's house, and the two studied together at the dining room table. Her parents were cordial to the boy. His own parents were inordinately proud of their son's choice in a girlfriend. It seemed like a perfect match, the kind that provokes jealousy in some people.

Something there is that cannot bear a perfect relationship and wants to drag it in the mud.

Which might have been the reason that three weeks before the prom, a rumor went around town that the two of them had spent Saturday night together in Cranfield at the motel on the highway. The rumor first appeared in a whispered conversation between two of the junior girls. One of them said that she had heard from a third party—"I can't say who"– that Don and Carla were seen driving toward Cranfield, and they didn't come home that night. Early Sunday morning Carla was seen getting out of her car at her house. Don was nowhere around.

"Probably she already let him out somewhere," the girl surmised. "Anyway, don't tell anyone I told you."

The other girl promised not to say a word, and in five minutes she was on the phone with the story to her best friend.

"Did you hear? Don and Carla spent the night at Cranfield at that motel on the highway! I just heard it from a reliable source that I can't name. But you can bet it's for real."

"My God! Are you sure? Why would her folks allow it?"

"I bet they didn't know anything about it," her informant said. "She probably made up some story about staying at a girlfriend's house or something. Anyway, Miss Prim and Proper isn't so perfect after all, is she?"

Throughout the day on Monday, several of the girls in the junior class refused to speak to Carla. She was perplexed and hurt by the snubs, and she talked with Myra about it. Myra, being Carla's friend, had been left out of the gossip. She knew no reason for the cold shoulders, but she promised to find out what she could.

Meanwhile, the entire basketball team cornered Don in the locker room and wanted details.

"Details? Of what?" Don asked.

"C'mon, man, give us the story. How'd you get her to say Yes?"

"What are you guys talking about?"

"Saturday night, Buddy. How'd you pull it off?"

"Listen," Don said, "Saturday night Carla and I went to a movie in Cranfield. She drove her dad's DeSoto, because my dad was out of town with our car. We got out of the movie around midnight . . . ."

"So, what'd ya see?" one of them interrupted.

"*The Desert Song.* What difference does that make? Anyway, her car wouldn't start. So we walked down the road to that motel and called her dad. He got Tom Pettit out of bed, and they came up. Something about the carburetor. It took him three hours to fix it. It was about four o'clock when we started back. She dropped me off at my house and went on home."

"If you say so."

"Man, that's a cool cover!" said another. "Now if her old man'll only swear to it, you got it made."

"I'm telling you, that's the truth. Now leave it alone!" Don was becoming angry.

"Sure, OK," they said, and left him.

When Don saw Carla after math class, she was visibly upset.

"We can't talk here," she said. "I'll call you later at home."

"Hey! Don't let those creeps get to you," he said.

About nine o'clock that evening, Don's phone rang.

"Can you talk?" It was Carla's voice; he could tell she had been crying.

"Sure. What's up?"

"Myra says there's a rumor going around that you and I spent the night together at the motel in Cranfield."

"I know," he answered. "Some of the guys jumped me about it. I tried to explain what happened, but they'd rather believe the rumor." He paused and heard her sniffle. "Listen, Babe, all we have to do is just go on being ourselves. We know we didn't do anything wrong. Eventually, it'll just die out."

Carla was quiet for a while, then she said, "I hope you're right. Maybe we ought to talk with Mr. Parsons."

"I don't know what he can do," Don answered. "But we can if you want to."

Carla said, "I'll see you at school tomorrow, OK?"

"Sure, Babe. Try not to worry about it anymore. It'll blow over. G'night."

The next morning Carla met Myra on the way to school. They entered the building together, passing a group of girls who stopped talking until they were inside.

"Who started this rumor anyhow?" Carla asked.

"I don't know," Myra said. "It seems to be all over the school. Like measles or something. But listen, you and Don need to just forget about it. If you let it get to you, it'll be like it was true, you know? Don't give 'em any hint that you're upset. Just let it go."

"That's hard to do, with the prom coming up."

The election for prom king and queen was scheduled for the Tuesday before the event, and Don and Carla had been odds-on favorites to win.

Two other boys and two other girls had been put forward as candidates by school clubs. Now with the rumor polluting the school's thinking, the election seemed like a free-for-all.

Walter VanDyke got home from work that afternoon earlier than he had expected, so Carla had a chance to talk. She called both her parents into the living room and sat down in front of them.

"There's something I need to tell you," she began. Tears filled her eyes. "There's a rumor going around at school that Don and I spent Saturday night together at the motel in Cranfield."

She broke down and sobbed.

"Listen, Honey" her father said, "things like this happen everywhere—even in the business world. If you let them get to you, you give them power over you. The best thing for you and Don to do is simply not respond. Just let it go in one ear and out the other. Pretty soon, you won't hear any more about it."

"That's what Myra said," Carla sniffed. "I just hope you're right. Sometimes kids can be so mean!"

By Wednesday the gossip had escalated into a vendetta against the most envied couple in Thornburg. Catcalls and vulgar remarks followed Carla as she left the building after class, hurled from the anonymity of the crowd descending the front steps. She did not acknowledge them. Myra caught up with her and slipped her arm in her friend's arm, and together they walked to Carla's house. As they came in the front door, Evelyn handed her daughter the telephone. "It's Don," she said.

"Hi," Carla said softly, as though to hide the conversation from the town.

"Hey, listen," Don said, "How about we get away for a couple hours? Why don't I pick you up, and we'll go for a drive—just to relax?"

"I don't know," she said. "Myra's here, and I just want to stay home a while. Could we go out later?"

"Sure. Maybe after supper? How about ice cream at the drive-in at Conger?"

"OK," she sighed. "I'll call you after supper."

When Don picked her up at 7:30, Carla told him she had to be home by ten.

"I just wish I knew who started this whole mess," she said.

"I'm afraid I'd punch somebody out if I knew," Don said.

"That's not the way to handle it, and you know it. We'll just keep on being ourselves, and maybe it'll all blow over, like you said."

They were driving north on Main Street, heading for Conger about seven miles away, when Dale Prentiss saw them and honked his horn. He pulled in behind them, his arm around a girl. As they passed the pool hall, others yelled at them and jumped into cars to follow. By the time Don and Carla got to the interstate, three carloads of kids were chasing them, honking their horns and yelling insults that made Carla roll up her window. Tears rolled down her face as she said, "Won't it ever stop?"

Don crossed the interstate and continued north toward Conger. The other cars followed. Dale got close enough to Don's car to bump his rear bumper. Don sped up to keep ahead of him. Dale only increased his speed. So did the others in the cars behind them.

"This is insane," Don said, and he pushed the accelerator to the floor. The car leaped forward, and the procession behind them raced to keep up.

"Don, just stop!" Carla said. "Somebody's going to get killed. Let's just stop and talk to them. Maybe that'll be enough to make them quit."

"They aren't gonna quit just by talking," Don said.

He was driving well past the speed limit now, trying to think what to do, when an animal suddenly crossed the road in front of him. He stamped on the brake while swerving to avoid it, and Dale's car ran into him, pushing Don's car sideways and into the ditch. It rolled onto its left side as it dropped off the highway. Dale's car skidded into it, pushing it on over. Carla was thrown against the dashboard, then on top of Don, then into the backseat as the car slammed into a tree.

The other two cars managed to stop without hitting them. Three or four of the boys jumped out and ran to the scene of the accident. They looked in the windows of the overturned car and saw Don bleeding from his face and arms. Carla lay unconscious on the ceiling of the car, her left arm broken and lying at a strange angle across her face.

Dale's red convertible sat upright, still on the road, but the girl with him had hit the windshield. Blood ran down her face. Dale seemed to be OK. He climbed out to see how Don and Carla were. He had hardly taken a step when he fainted in the road. A girl from one of the other cars ran to him, trembling and crying. Others came up; one went to the girl in Dale's car.

"Somebody go back to town and get the ambulance up here!" one of the boys shouted. The last car in the lineup made a U-turn and headed back to town.

A boy wrenched open the driver's door of Don's car and froze. Don looked up at him. His face was ashen white, and he mumbled, "Where's Carla?"

"Sh-she's here, she's in the back seat," the boy said. He was trembling now, nearly unable to speak.

"We oughta get 'em out of there," another boy said. "What if the car blows up?"

Two boys helped Don out of the car and laid him on the grass in the ditch. Then they opened the rear door, carefully, because Carla was lying against it. Cradling her head in their hands, and taking care not to move her arm, four or five of them lifted her out of the car and laid her beside Don. The entire group gathered around them. Some of the girls were crying and saying, "Oh Carla, I'm so sorry!"

"You're gonna be OK," one of the boys said. "Kenny went after the ambulance. They'll be here in a minute. Just lay still."

Carla's eyes were still shut, and Don seemed to be in shock. Dale had revived by now. His girlfriend sat with him against the side of the car, dabbing her eyes with a Kleenex someone had offered her. She held a handkerchief to her head to stop the bleeding.

"Doesn't anybody know first aid?" someone asked.

"Just keep 'em warm, and don't move 'em any more than you have to," one of the boys said. He reached into Don's car and turned off the key. A girl from the third car brought a blanket and spread it over the injured couple. Several cried quietly. The boys walked aimlessly on the roadway, looking anxiously in the direction of Thornburg, when a red light flashed in the distance.

"Hey, it's the ambulance!" one said. He took off his shirt and began waving it in the air. The ambulance drew to a stop near the overturned car as Marshal Bates drove up behind it. Two paramedics ran to the couple in the ditch. They took vital signs, noted Carla's broken arm, and put it in an immobilizing cuff. Then they treated both for shock and tended to the cuts on Don's face and arms. When the pair were stable enough to be moved, they lifted them onto stretchers and put them into the ambulance. They treated the cuts on the second girl's face and bandaged them, then turned the ambulance back toward the interstate and the county hospital.

"Well!" the marshal sighed, "who can tell me what happened?"

Several at once, then one at a time, the group tried to explain the accident as caused by an animal that had run onto the road.

"How fast were you going?"

"Prob'ly faster than we should have," admitted one of the boys.

"Yep," said the marshal, "this kind of accident doesn't happen when people are following at a safe distance and driving at a reasonable speed. Where were you all going in such a hurry?"

A brief dead silence followed this question. One of the girls said lamely, "We were just following them."

"Yeah, just havin' a little fun," a boy said.

"You call this fun?" the marshal said. The group was silent. "Well, two kids who have been the victims of some pretty nasty rumors this past week are going to be in the hospital tonight, because some of you thought it would be fun to harass them. I want all of your names, and I want statements from all of you. We're going back into town and get these cars off the highway. I'll send a wrecker for Don's car. Then I want to see you in my office. Understood?"

They all nodded and a few said, "Yes, Sir."

Don and Carla were in school on the following Monday. Her left arm was in a cast; Don had a bandage across his nose and a few healing scratches. Other than that they seemed normal. Don's teammates said they were glad to see him back in school. Ray Spencer, junior class president, made a point of telling Don that he was glad to see him and sorry about the accident and the rumor.

"I knew there was nothing to it," he said. "You guys are still tops in my book."

Myra, who had sat by Carla's bedside in the hospital all Wednesday night with the VanDykes, and had driven back to the hospital the next afternoon, hardly let her out of sight now. The other girls seemed hesitant to initiate conversation with Carla, but when she spoke to them they responded with interest in her condition. A few signed her cast. Two said they were sorry about the accident. No one mentioned the rumor.

The vote for prom king and queen took place on Tuesday. Don and Carla were elected by a landslide.

"Hard to top that for a campaign strategy," one of the teachers remarked to a colleague, then said, "I'm sorry, that was out of line."

The prom was a huge success. The band was wonderful, if volume is any indication, and Don and Carla looked radiant as they took their "thrones."

Thornburg still talks about that prom, and about what a great family Don and Carla have raised: three beautiful children who are intelligent and well behaved.

And "Aunt Myra" and her husband Ray Spencer, who live next door to them, are frequent guests in their home.

The Great Fourth of July Bank Robbery

The Midwestern Bank in Thornburg, Indiana, had been built in the 1920s from Indiana limestone as a fortress against robbers and a monument to the town's financial stability. It stood prominently on the southwest corner of Main and Jefferson Streets. Its steel vault was set in the basement to discourage theft. The outside doors of the building were heavy oak backed by iron grating. A new vault with lockboxes was installed in the late '40s on the main floor for the greater convenience of the tellers and customers. Only once in its thirty-four years had the interior décor been enhanced, and that was a simple repainting of the walls from Federal Gold to a more welcoming Coastal Blue.

The bank had not failed in the Great Depression, because the citizens of Thornburg had faith in Perry Rutherford, the bank's president, and they left their money there. Mr. Rutherford lived in Devington Circle, next door to Mrs. Devington. A widower, he was the bank's only president since its beginning. His brown fedora was his trademark; he wore it winter and summer. He was a small man, quiet, and fanatic about details. His employees respected and admired him, but never once did any of them presume upon his friendship or his need for privacy. He was always pleasant but never chatty. And he was scrupulously honest, to the point of offense when unavoidable.

It was the custom of the town to ask Mr. Rutherford to ride in the lead car of every Fourth-of-July parade as the Grand Marshal. He seemed to enjoy the honor, waving to the folks sitting on either side of Main Street. The parade proceeded north from its gathering place in the field behind Clayton's Funeral Home at the south end of town to the high school on the north end, turned west, then south on Pike Street to end at the starting place.

It seemed that Thornburg paraded every moveable vehicle it owned: late model convertibles, Ed Porter's 1928 Model A Ford, several tractors pulling hay wagons loaded with the various graduating classes from the high school, even the town ambulance with its red light flashing and an occasional siren wail. The Freemasons marched behind the members of the Town Council, carrying their lodge flag. The high school band could usually be assembled to provide some Sousa marches. A couple who lived in the country south of town sometimes dressed in western garb and rode at the end of the parade, firing blanks from pearl-handled revolvers. It was a show the entire town anticipated with excitement every year.

People chose their places along Main Street early in the day, sitting on folding chairs and drinking coffee, chatting with one another, awaiting the starting announcement from the judges' stand in front of Poteet's Dry Cleaning business. The electrical hookups were easier there, a central location from which the judges could view the parade.

The Lions Club chose a Sight Queen during each year's festivities. The girls rode on the backs of convertibles and gave the "Miss America

Wave" to the crowds, swiveling their hands on their wrists until they thought they would fall off. The girls were judged by votes cast in the weeks before the parade, each vote costing a penny. The girl who collected the most votes won. The money went into the Lions Club Sight Fund.

The Fourth-of-July that year was sweltering. The TV weatherman forecast a high of ninety-two degrees with a clear sky. By ten o'clock a burning sun baked the crowd sitting along the streets, some raising umbrellas against the heat. The starting field began to fill with entries. Town Council President Betty Allison arrived in George Pattison's maroon Hudson convertible. The band wore the only uniforms they had: 100% wool for marching in football season. Already they were sweating and sucking on lemons to stave off thirst and fainting. The majorettes in their short skirts and white boots were the leading edge of the band, and every boy in the first row of trumpets secretly hoped to catch one when she fainted from the heat.

Promptly at ten o'clock the judges announced the start of the parade. The American Legion Post carried the colors ahead of the band, which played the National Anthem. People along the streets stood with their hands over their hearts; a few sang the words. Then the band broke into "The Stars and Stripes Forever." A new white Chevrolet convertible provided by Harley Cross, the local Chevrolet dealer, with the seventy-seven-year old Mr. Rutherford in the front seat, followed, and the parade was under way.

It was the longest, if not the best parade in the town's history. The mail delivery truck, both police cars, the two fire trucks with the rescue van, the street sweeper, and even the garbage truck were all parts of the procession. The garbage truck had been recently painted a lime green and was washed to look good for the occasion. By 10:15 the Sight

Queen candidates had all passed the judges' stand. The new Chevy convertible with Mr. Rutherford in the front seat had arrived just opposite Bennett's Park on Pike Street, when Mr. Rutherford slumped forward against the dashboard. The driver immediately stopped the car, holding up his hand for the vehicles behind him to halt. A bystander ran back to the ambulance to tell the driver to come up to the lead car.

Emergency medical technicians leaped out and opened the car door to find Mr. Rutherford unconscious. They lifted him out, laid him on the collapsible gurney from the ambulance, and tried to resuscitate him. He regained consciousness, but seemed unable to speak. His entire right side was unresponsive.

"I think he's had a stroke," one of the techs said. "Let's get him to the hospital."

They put him in the ambulance, pulled around the band, who were now standing with their instruments along the curb, and headed for the hospital in the county seat. Miss Cates, one of the tellers at the bank, lived on Pike Street. She watched her boss loaded into the ambulance, then went up and down Main Street until she found the vice-president, Mr. Bowles, and told him the news. Mr. Bowles immediately went home to get his car and drove to the hospital. The parade finished with little joy or fanfare. The worried participants talked of little else than Mr. Rutherford's health. The crowd took their chairs home, and the Fourth-of-July Parade was over.

Meanwhile, Mr. Rutherford's condition was pronounced stable. Mr. Bowles called Miss Cates from the hospital and asked her to go to the bank—"You do have a key, don't you?"—and find Mr. Rutherford's checkbook. "It'll be in the top drawer of his desk; he's worried about it being left there. He scribbled that on a piece of paper with his left hand, poor guy!"

"I don't have a key to his office," she said.

"There's one in my desk," Bowles said. "You can use that."

She went immediately to the bank to find the checkbook. Opening the front door, she could see through to the rear door. It was standing partly open. She gasped and went quickly to it. It had been broken into, its deadbolt sawn through and its jamb splintered. The iron grate had been pried away from the frame. She ran back to the vault to see if it was safe. The huge door was standing open. Entering, she could see that the drawers in which they stored the cash were open and empty, but their locks had not been broken. She suddenly remembered Mr. Rutherford's checkbook and hurried to find the key. She felt like an intruder as she opened Mr. Rutherford's desk. Nothing had been disturbed in the room.

She put the checkbook into her purse, then picked up the phone and called Marshal Bates. She told him of the break-in and the missing money. He asked her to stay there. He arrived in less than a minute— he had only to cross the corner—and began to inspect the damage.

"Now this is strange," he said, looking at the vault. "No sign of forced entry here, and yet the back door was broken into. Whoever did this knew something about the vault"–here he looked at Miss Cates— "and probably had the combination."

"Marshal, you're not suggesting that one of us in the bank had something to do with this!"

"All I'm sayin', Miss Cates, is that it looks suspicious. How could a stranger open that vault unless he had the combination? Someone must have given it to him."

"But if they did that, why wouldn't they also have given him a key to the back door?"

"Good question," the marshal replied. He looked around the bank for any signs that might give clues to the thief's identity and made some notes on a pad he carried. He and Miss Cates went out and locked the front door.

"Seems kinda silly," he said, "locking this door while the other one stands open. I'll get Charlie Smith and Ed Porter to come over here and see if they can fix that door—at least temporarily."

Folks seeing Miss Cates and Marshal Bates coming out of the bank on a holiday began to ask questions. It was soon all over town that the bank had been robbed.

"Heaven only knows how much money was taken!" exclaimed Beatrice Lyons. "I just hope they didn't get into my lockbox. I've got my mother's diamond ring in there; if anything happened to it I'd just die!"

She was assured that the lockboxes had been left untouched. Apparently all the thief was after was cash. A detective agency was called in, and the bank examiners showed up the next morning. There was no doubt that the rear door had been broken into from the outside; dirt on the floor leading from it to the vault showed the thief's intent. But just how he was able to open the vault remained a mystery.

"It must have happened while the parade was going on," the marshal surmised. "Most of the town would have been watching the parade, and the bank's back door is hidden by the back side of the newspaper office. It wouldn't have taken long for someone with a crowbar and a hacksaw to get in. Nobody would have heard him because of the band and the sirens and all. He cut the wires to the alarm."

"You think it was just one man?" the examiner asked.

"Looks that way," the detective answered. "Only one set of footprints, and only one useable fingerprint near the door. Probably an amateur, from the mess he made of that door. Should be easy to catch. I'll do some calling around. These jobs have an M.O. that's pretty obvious."

Miss Cates and Elizabeth Joiner, another teller, agreed that Mr. Rutherford should not be told of the robbery until he was strong enough to bear the news. Maybe by that time the thief would be caught and the money recovered. "I think the news might just kill him," Miss Cates said, and Elizabeth agreed.

During the next twenty-four hours it was determined that $156,000 were missing. The bank examiner had found the books in order. No other keys were out except those in the keeping of Miss Cates and Mr. Bowles. The detective took statements from each of them. There was only one other employee, a part-time teller named James McClure, and he was out of town for the holiday.

"Well!" exclaimed a woman at the drug store the next day. "It seems to me they ought to be looking for that kid they hired, that McClure boy. Where does he live, anyway?"

"Over on Barton Road," her friend said. "I don't think he's even twenty-one yet. Hardly dry behind the ears. What business does he have handling people's money?"

"I never go to him. Always go to the other two," the first woman said.

"Me too. Well, I just hope they catch the culprit before anything worse happens in this town!"

Meanwhile, the detective agency had been hard at work, turning up some leads that bore fruit. A known thief from a nearby town was questioned. He denied knowing anything about the robbery, and he had a solid alibi. He said it looked like the work of Eddy Longworth, who had robbed a bank over in Ohio once and got away with it.

"The law ain't so smart after all, are they?" he sneered.

"Where can I find this Eddy Longworth?" the detective asked.

"I don't know. He moves around a lot."

The name was put on the police network. In less than a day Eddy Longworth had been picked up in Indianapolis and questioned about the robbery. He denied it, of course, but his fingerprint matched the one found by the door, and he could not account for his presence on July 4, with any credible alibi. He was transported to the county jail, and a trial date was set. No amount of questioning could get him to change his story: He had broken into the bank, yes, but when he got to the vault, it was open, and there was no money inside. He left the way he had come, down the back alley, mingled with the parade crowd, and left town.

A trial date was set for September, and business in Thornburg went back to normal. The bank's insurance company was hesitant to pay for the loss until after the trial, hoping that Eddy Longworth could be plea-bargained into divulging the hiding place of the money. His attorney pointed out that the vault had not been forced, that Eddy would have had to work with someone in the bank to gain the combination. He moved for a delay of the trial until sufficient evidence could be found linking a bank employee to Eddy Longworth. The judge was against a delay on the grounds of a full docket. He was eager to put Eddy away for a while; he denied the motion.

Meanwhile, James McClure was contacted at his grandparents' home in Wooster, Ohio. He denied any knowledge of the theft or of Eddy Longworth. The detective thought he should be brought back for questioning, but Marshal Bates pointed out that there was no more evidence linking him with the theft than there was with any other bank employee.

Three weeks after the disappearance of the money, Miss Cates and Mr. Bowles went to visit Mr. Rutherford in the hospital. He had made enough improvement that the doctor thought he could stand to hear the news of the robbery—especially since Eddy Longworth was in jail, and it seemed to be only a matter of time before he could be persuaded to trade the $156,000 for his freedom.

Mr. Rutherford was eating lunch when they arrived, feeding himself with his left hand. The nurse told them he was making progress every day, that his speech had returned "really well." With his bed cranked up to a half-sitting position, he had just finished his Jello pudding when the two visitors entered the room.

"Well, well!" he said. He laid down his spoon.

"How are you, Mr. Rutherford? Looks like you're eating well," Miss Cates said.

"They feeding you good, Mr. Rutherford?" Bowles asked.

"Oh, yes," he answered. His speech was still slurred, but intelligible.

The two employees told him the small news of the town before they got around to mentioning the robbery.

"Mr. Rutherford, there's something we think you ought to know," Bowles said. "During the parade on July 4, there was a break-in at the bank, and the vault was opened. We don't know just how it was done, because it didn't seem to be forced in any way. None of the lockboxes were broken into, but the back door of the bank was jimmied. They caught the fellow who did it. I'm afraid he got $156,000. We haven't recovered the money yet. But don't worry, we will. It's just a matter of time."

Mr. Rutherford had a strange look on his face, all the stranger for his stroke, which pulled one side of his face down. He chuckled as he said, "I'm sorry. I forgot."

"What did you forget, Mr. Rutherford?"

He turned his face toward the two of them and said, "That fellow might have broken into the bank, but he didn't get any money."

"The vault was open, Sir," Miss Cates said, "and the money is gone."

Mr. Rutherford chuckled again. "Well, it didn't go far. Sorry, I must've forgotten to close the vault. I put the money in the old vault downstairs the night before the parade for safekeeping. Y'know, it always seems to me that holidays are prime times for robberies, folks being away and all and not on their guard. The money's in the old vault, safe and sound."

Miss Cates looked at him in stunned silence. Finally she asked, "Where is the combination to the old vault?"

"Right here in my checkbook," Mr. Rutherford said. He patted the drawer of his bedside table. "Thanks for bringing it up. Now you take these numbers—he opened the drawer and took out the checkbook—and go open that old vault, and put the money back where it belongs."

He gave them the numbers, which Miss Cates wrote down, and thanked them for coming.

"I'll see you in a couple of weeks," he said as they left.

"Well, that is the most . . . ! I never thought to look down there," Miss Cates said as they left the hospital.

"Wouldn't have done us any good without this combination," Bowles replied.

He and Miss Cates drove to the bank and went downstairs to the old vault. Mr. Bowles opened it, using the numbers Mr. Rutherford had given them.

The vault was empty. They stared in silence until Mr. Bowles said, "Why, how can this be? He said he put the money in here himself."

He looked steadily at Miss Cates. "Are you sure you don't have the combination to this vault?"

Miss Cates was shocked by the implications of the question. "Mr. Bowles, I have *never* had this combination!" Her eyes were wide open, her chin trembled. "I was hired after the new vault was installed, you might remember!"

"Now, now," Bowles said, "I didn't mean to imply that you took the money. I just thought that maybe another copy of the combination existed that someone might have got their hands on."

"Well, you can put your mind at ease on that score, Mr. Bowles," said Miss Cates in a huff.

"And I'm sure Elizabeth doesn't have it either. She came to work after I did."

"What about the McClure boy?" Bowles asked. "Couldn't he have had access to Mr. Rutherford's office, maybe gone through his things until he found the combination?"

"Mr. Bowles, I don't believe any of our employees would do such a thing!" exclaimed Miss Cates. "There has to be some other explanation. Besides, Mr. Rutherford never leaves his office unlocked."

After a space of silence Bowles said, "I'm afraid I know what happened."

"What on earth?"

Bowles looked grave as he answered. "Either our Mr. Rutherford is getting senile, or he has pulled off a very slick bank robbery. I mean, who would suspect him? He's a paragon of virtue in the community."

"Oh, Mr. Bowles! That's just not possible!" Miss Cates said. "I've know him for most of my life. He couldn't do such a thing!"

"Well, we have only his word that he put the money in here. And it's obviously gone. I wonder if that Eddy Longworth has told us the whole story."

"But, there were only Mr. Rutherford's fingerprints on the vault upstairs," said Miss Cates.

"A clever thief might wear gloves," said Bowles.

"But surely he couldn't have had *both* combinations," argued Miss Cates.

"That's what makes me wonder."

Miss Cates stared at Bowles and shook her head slowly from side to side. "You just *can't* think that Mr. Rutherford would do this!"

Bowles walked out of the vault without answering. He and Miss Cates closed the heavy door, spinning the combination lock to secure it.

"I just had another thought," Mr. Bowles said. "Who were the former employees of the bank? Couldn't one of them have kept the combination to the old vault and come in after the back door was broken in?"

"That still doesn't explain the new vault being open," said Miss Cates.

"Well, if Mr. Rutherford had opened it, like he said, and put the money in the old vault, he might simply have forgotten to close the new vault. He said so himself."

"He did say he might have," Miss Cates agreed.

"My point exactly!" said Bowles. "He's just not the brilliant mind he was for so many years. What a pity! I wonder if he has the money at home. He could have absentmindedly taken it home, don't you think?"

Miss Cates could only shake her head. "We ought to tell the marshal what we've found."

Marshal Bates was out of town for the day, the desk sergeant said, but he would have him contact Mr. Bowles in the morning. Ted Bates came to the bank the next morning in the company of two other men: one a representative of the bank's insurance company, the other the county prosecutor. He knocked on Mr. Bowles's door.

"Good morning, Elwood," the Marshal said. "May we have a minute?"

"Why, uh, certainly!" Bowles said. "Come in." He indicated chairs for the three men. "What have you found out?"

"Well, quite a bit," Ted said. "Oh, let me introduce Mr. Baines from the insurance company, and the County Prosecutor, Charles Portman."

Bowles smiled weakly as he shook their hands. The three men sat down.

"I spent yesterday in Fort Wayne," the marshal began. "I visited several banks, where I found accounts in the name of Perry H. Rutherford totaling $156,000. The money was deposited in four banks, some in CDs and some in checking accounts. I have copies of the signature cards; they've been analyzed by a handwriting expert in the police department there. So there's no longer any doubt about where the money went."

"Oh, mercy!" exclaimed Bowles. "Mr. Rutherford a thief! Why, that's . . . that's not possible!"

"Exactly what I thought," the marshal returned. "Someone would have to have taken the cards to him in the hospital and got his signature. With his right hand not working too well, I could imagine they'd be pretty scratchy. But these looked a lot like his old signature here at the bank."

"Well, I suppose he could have set this all up before the robbery," Bowles said. "You know, got the cards and opened the accounts before the fourth."

"Miss Cates tells me he was at the bank every day for a week before the fourth. And the money wasn't deposited until the seventh day of the month, while Mr. Rutherford was still in the hospital, pretty much incapacitated."

"But, you said you had the signatures analyzed, and they proved that Mr. Rutherford had deposited the money. He must have had an accomplice."

"I didn't say what the analysis showed," Marshal Bates replied.

"Well, what *did* it show?"

"That the signatures had been forged," Bates said. "They didn't match Mr. Rutherford's signature taken from documents here at the bank."

"You mean, someone took the money from the vault and deposited it in Ft. Wayne under Mr. Rutherford's name?" Bowles pursued. "Why, that would have required someone to have the combination to the old vault."

"Yep," Ted said. "And to leave the new vault open to make it look like a break-in. And to wipe off any fingerprints. They just weren't thinking far enough. Only a bank employee could have opened that vault. Only a bank employee with access to the combinations to both vaults. Someone who knew that Mr. Rutherford had written them inside his checkbook. And the three tellers had no access to Mr. Rutherford's office unless he was there. He told me so himself."

Mr. Bowles looked at his desk, then he looked at the three men before him. "So, uh, you suspect someone at the bank."

"Elwood, you're the only person who could have had access to Mr. Rutherford's checkbook. As vice-president, you had a key to his office. He told me so. He trusted you completely."

Bowles was silent. At last he said quietly, "It—it was just for safekeeping, until this could all be straightened out. I thought the money would be safer in Fort Wayne. I didn't think it was necessary to tell anyone. It was just for a short time."

"But some of the CDs were for five years," the Marshal answered. "How long did you expect it to take?"

"But Mr. Rutherford . . . ." Bowles began, "uh, has been showing signs of aging lately, and when he put the money in the old vault on the night of the third of July, I had just come by to get some papers I had left on my desk. I saw him open the vault and take out the money, then he went downstairs and put it in the old vault. I didn't question him about it, but it looked to me like a mark of paranoia. I thought the money would be safer in other banks until we could persuade him to retire. You see my point?"

"What was the purpose of putting the money in four different banks, then?" Ted pursued.

"If it was only until the Board of Directors could take action, shouldn't you have told them? And wouldn't one bank have been enough to hold it until then? No, Elwood, you saw a chance to steal the money and let Mr. Rutherford take the blame, didn't you? As far as you were concerned, his stroke was just a stroke of good luck."

"Mr. Bowles," the prosecutor said, "I'm afraid I'm going to have to ask Marshal Bates to remand you into the custody of the county until a trial can be set. You'll be charged with theft and counterfeiting a signature."

"You mean, *arrest* me!" Bowles shouted. He stood up behind his desk with all the self-righteousness he could muster and demanded that he be allowed to contact his attorney immediately.

"Oh, you'll need a lawyer all right," the prosecutor said. "You can make the call from the county jail." He stood, and the others joined him.

"I'm sorry, Elwood," Ted said. "It's best if we go together in my car." He indicated the door.

Bowles walked slowly around his desk and followed the marshal into the main lobby. Two or three customers and both tellers stared as the four men left the bank.

"I wonder what's up?" Elizabeth Joiner said to Miss Cates.

"I don't know," Miss Cates replied. "Mr. Bowles didn't look too well, did he?"

The trial followed Eddy Longworth's by a week. The Board of Directors and several other town members were present. The jury returned the verdict, "Guilty as charged." The sentence was set at five years in a medium security prison.

Mr. Rutherford returned to his office the following week, pale but functional. A long-time member of the board was elected to fill Mr. Bowles's position. The money was retrieved from Fort Wayne and put back into the main vault, and the back door was replaced with one a lot more burglar proof.

Mr. Rutherford lived ten more years, riding in the lead car of every Fourth-of-July parade.

But now he held a large umbrella as protection against the mid-summer sun.

Clarence's Christmas Conflagration

Christmas in Thornburg has always been high celebration. Citizens who have not stood out among their fellow townsfolk have a chance to shine at Christmas. Literally. Because the town has an annual lighting contest, and neighbors try to outdo each other in creative displays of house and yard lights, manger scenes, Santas on rooftops with reindeer and sleigh, and an annual drain on the town's electrical power supply. Ed Porter begins to stock Christmas lights and paraphernalia in early November, because he knows that by the first or second week in December it will be gone.

In the early years of the 1950s, most of the sensational displays were confined to the wealthier homes, such as those in Devington Circle. In later years, other citizens put forth considerable expense to compete for the town's prize of $100 and whatever public acclaim a town like Thornburg could muster. The Abbots sent their twins up a ladder to string lights along the roofline and set a lighted Santa Claus by the chimney. Bill Carrington and his wife Barb bought a fabulous manger scene from Frankenmuth, Michigan, which graced the southeast corner of Wood and Maple Streets. Folks out for an evening walk would stand and gaze in awe at its lifelike figures.

The house on the southeast corner of Main and Washington Streets belonged to Clarence and Pauline Cobb. They rarely decorated at Christmas. Their only son lived on his own in Indianapolis, where he worked for a plumber. Clarence was a volatile sort of person, impulsive and given to manic episodes that usually resulted in laughter for the town and embarrassment to himself. Pauline was quiet and withdrawn, keeping to herself much of the time. She sometimes cleaned houses in town for extra money. People who knew her best said that she was not a well person, but they couldn't be more specific.

Once, two vehicles collided at their intersection. Clarence bolted from his front door, running to the scene of the accident wearing only his shorts. Suddenly discovering his condition, he raced back to the house, returning almost immediately, hauling up his trousers as he ran. He was barefooted and got a piece of broken glass in his foot, and had to go to Dr. Call to have it cared for. It was typical of Clarence. He worked at the lumberyard for Bill Meyers. As long as Bill kept an eye on him, Clarence was fine. He loaded lumber into pickups, helped sort the studs into "straight" and "bent," and generally kept the yard clean for the trucks that came through.

He was an eager employee, and Bill gave him more responsibility as Clarence seemed ready to take it on. Sometimes he worked at the counter taking orders and talking with customers about their projects. Folks who knew him got along well with him, but those who had few dealings with him were sometimes put off by his manner and remarks. On one occasion, rather than tell a customer his paneling had not yet come in, Clarence told him they had to quit carrying it because it had worms in it. The customer told Bill later that he would buy his lumber someplace else rather than deal with Clarence. Bill put Clarence back in the yard stacking lumber.

Bill and Dana Meyers went to Florida for the month of December every year and left Clarence in charge. He got along all right with it, because there seemed to be little construction going on at that time of year. He sold a few things from time to time, but the lumberyard was pretty much shut down in the winter months. One January he undertook to paint the interior of the office. "Just to use up that purple paint we couldn't get rid of," he later explained to Bill. They lived with the garish walls until spring, when Bill and his brother Phil covered the walls with two coats of a medium tan.

Early that summer, Pauline Cobb entered the hospital in the county seat for tests, which determined that she was suffering from a liver disease that had no cure. By August she was dead. Their son came home to spend some time with his father. His job required him two weeks later, and Clarence was left alone. The house seemed too big now; his footsteps echoed from the walls, ceiling, and floors, reminding him how bereft he was. He decided to sell the house and move in with his parents, who lived east of town on County Road 50 S about a mile from the lumberyard. They were in declining health, and Clarence felt bound to stay close to them.

He had few close friends, mostly other single men who used to sit around the lumberyard and smoke, chatting aimlessly about the weather and the local gossip. He seldom left town, and all Bill's efforts to cheer him up only emphasized his misery. Occasionally, he would walk down Main Street to Barclay's Restaurant for lunch while Bill kept the store. A few men were usually there at the back table, drinking coffee and eating pie, and Clarence would join them.

In late November, as the town bachelors and disenchanted husbands gathered at the table, the conversation turned to the Christmas decorations already in evidence on several properties. They talked of the $100 prize and who would probably get it. For two years in a row, Carl Purcell in Devington Circle had claimed the prize for the most creative display. He had outlined his house in lights, put an extensive scene of Santa and the elves on his front lawn, and hung lights and garlands from the rows of evergreens that separated his yard from the others. The group speculated what it would take to outdo him. At that moment, Clarence Cobb knew how to handle his depression.

The day Bill and Dana left for Florida, Clarence went up into his parents' attic and brought down all the family Christmas ornaments that had been accumulating over half a century. He loaded them into his pickup and drove to the lumberyard. Then he began to hang them on every available protrusion he could find. The interior of the building soon filled up with decorations, so he went outside and hung them on the eaves, the window sills, the banisters on either side of the steps, even on the racks that held the lumber out in the yard. Everything that had been part of his family Christmases for fifty years went up someplace. He stood across the road and surveyed his handiwork. It looked festive and marvelous to him. But it still lacked something.

Now he went back to the attic and brought down boxes of lights from the early 1940s, bubble lights from the early '50s, and all the strands that had fallen into disuse because of burned-out bulbs or broken wires. He took all these to the lumber yard and repaired what he could. Painstakingly he hung them from the roof, the lumber racks out in the yard, even the piles of lumber themselves. As evening came on, he plugged in the extension cord that connected all these various strands of lights. The lumberyard suddenly came to life in an explosion of color. Clarence had not felt such joy in a long time. He walked out to the corner at Barton Road to view his masterpiece.

The scene exceeded his expectations. The very air surrounding the usually dull yard seemed to glow, illuminating everything around it. In ecstasy he ran down Barton Road to the houses below Washington Street, knocking on doors and calling people's attention to the beauty he had created. Folks obligingly "oohed" and "aahed" over his endeavor, then smiled to themselves as they said, "Well, Clarence, you really did it this time!"

As he stood on a front porch in the next block west, proudly showing off his creation to a family gathered at their front door, he noticed a brighter light than he had seen before. It seemed to grow by the minute. Then he saw flames above the roofline of the store and realized to his horror that the yard was on fire. The old Christmas lights must have had a short in them! Maybe a bare wire that he missed taping. Maybe a bad connection where sawdust got in. All these speculations went through his mind as he ran back to the lumberyard, panting from the cold and his fifty-one years.

By the time he reached the lumberyard, the entire stock of wood was in flames. The fire had not yet reached the building. He ran inside and called the fire department, then ran outside again and grabbed the only fire extinguisher he knew of, just inside the first bay of the yard. It had not been inspected for several years. He pressed the handle and heard only a slight fizz, then nothing. He threw it down and ran to get the hose that was connected to a spigot on the back of the building. It was not there! Bill must have put it away for the winter. Helplessly he stood, watching the conflagration consume the entire stock of lumber.

By now, people all over town could see the flames in the northeast. They stood on their porches and sidewalks, shivering, watching the fire and calling across front yards to their neighbors about what might have caused it.

One woman said, "It's purty, though, ain't it?"

In a few minutes the wail of the volunteer fire department siren filled the air. The town's two fire trucks rounded the corner at the lumberyard. Men jumped off and connected the hose to the hydrant at the corner and began spraying water on the flames. But it was too late to save the yard. They were able to douse the flames licking at the back of the store, so it was saved. But the lumber was gone. The firemen stayed for another half hour and soaked the embers to prevent a flare-up later. They tried to console Clarence, then went back to the station.

At his parents' home, Clarence called Bill Meyers in Florida and reported the disaster. Bill asked if Clarence was all right and if anyone else had been involved. Then he said,

"Clarence, I know it's a big loss, but I don't want you to take it personally. You did the best you could to make the place part of the Christmas celebration, and I bet the folks who saw it won't ever forget it. I'm just glad no one was hurt."

"But it's all gone, Bill," Clarence said in a voice verging on tears.

"Listen, Clarence," Bill said, "it's all insured. We can rebuild. Don't worry about it. It was an accident that could have happened to any house in town."

Clarence heard him chuckle to himself as he said, "I'm just sorry I wasn't there to see it."

At three o'clock in the afternoon of the day before Christmas, on the steps of the Town Hall, Council President Betty Allison announced the winner of the decorating contest: "For the third year in a row, the $100 prize goes to Mr. and Mrs. Carl Purcell of Devington Circle."

A ripple of applause from the few hardy souls who had ventured out in the cold to form an audience was barely audible in the snow and frost. Carl stepped up to receive his check from the town and said "Thank you," and went back to stand by his wife.

"Now this year," Betty continued, "we're awarding another prize: for the most unusual display of light—even though it lasted for only a few minutes. Clarence Cobb, would you come up here?"

Poor Clarence! As if he had not been humiliated enough already! He stumbled up the steps of the Town Hall, and Betty handed him an envelope.

"This is a check from the insurance company for the full amount of the loss of the Meyers Lumberyard," she said to the crowd. Muffled applause burst forth from mittened and gloved hands. Then she added, "And here's something for you, Clarence."

She turned around and signaled to her husband, who had been standing just inside the door of the Town Hall. He came forth carrying a large, bright red fire extinguisher and presented it to Clarence, who, for the first time since the fire, grinned.

"Merry Christmas, Clarence," Betty said, and all the people echoed the sentiment.

"Now someone else wants to say something," Betty announced, and stepped down. Out of the Town Hall came Bill and Dana Meyers.

Bill put an arm around Clarence's shoulder as he said, "I couldn't let you folks celebrate Christmas without me this year—especially since Clarence went to so much trouble to give you a good show." He grinned down at Clarence. "He's the only person who ever had the ambition to decorate our old lumberyard, and for a little while we really shined—all over town!"

Genial laughter ran through the crowd, and a few advanced to shake Clarence's hand. Bill Meyers had turned a Christmas tragedy into a new beginning: for the lumberyard and Clarence Cobb. In the spring the debris from the fire was cleared away, and the Meyers Lumberyard was rebuilt. Clarence's son came home to Thornburg to help with the business; he and his father worked in the lumberyard together. And the first thing folks noticed when they visited the newly renovated business was the presence of a new fire extinguishing system, with automatic overhead sprinklers in every bay of the yard.

The Craft Fair

Every August the Thornburg Women's Quilting and Knitting Circle held a craft fair. Not all the entries were fabric. Some were papermache, some were wood, and one summer a crèche made of baked dough showed up. Someone offered the opinion that Joseph looked a bit crusty. But the majority were quilts or sweaters and scarves (matching of course), and some needlepoint. Elnora Devington was the president of the circle, assisted in her annual organization of the event by Barbara Parsons, the principal's wife, and Melvia Markham, wife of the Methodist minister. The top three entries were judged Grand Prize, Second, and Third Prize and auctioned off at the close of the fair. The money went into a scholarship fund for high school graduates.

Mary Lucille Poteet had been a member of the circle for twelve years and had never won a prize. Her particular craft was weaving and knitting; she worked diligently at her loom to produce homemade rugs. They were made of heavy material such as denim or corduroy, and while they were serviceable, they were not what the other members of the circle considered art. Her knitting came closer to what the circle expected. Mary Lucille had entered a layette one year made of a light blue yarn, and though it did not win a prize, a lady from Cranfield bought it. So Mary Lucille was encouraged to pursue knitting as her entry for the next year's fair.

Her husband, Emmett, was a large man, bald, and built like a drop of heavy weight oil. And he stuttered. Emmett ran the dry cleaning business in town. It was known that his wife made his cotton flannel nightshirts, which he wore year-round, and that she and her husband slept in separate rooms. Mary Lucille did not hide the fact: "He snores like a hog," she told the women. The ladies of the Quilting and Knitting Circle sniffed and declined any knowledge of what a snoring hog sounded like.

There was no doubt, either in Thornburg or Cranfield or Conger, that the quilts produced by this gifted group of women were superior to those of nearly any others in the county. Collectors regularly showed up at the fair to buy them. Each year they seemed more complex and beautiful. The grand prize nearly always went to one of these exquisitely crafted quilts; second and third prizes were often divided among the knitted garments. The only prize given to an entry not made of fabric in some form was a third prize for Terry Manning's creation of his family farm, rendered in three kinds of wood. Actual hay bales no larger than a pea were stacked on a tiny wagon; a flock of minuscule chickens pecked in the barnyard. They were made of pieces of feather glued to wooden beads, with beaks of quill from the feathers' points. It was condescendingly supposed that the prize was awarded because Terry was only twelve, and his mother was a member of the circle.

Such leniency, unknown in former years, must have been the encouragement Mary Lucille needed to venture upon the project that occupied her during the months of spring and early summer. Melvia Markham, visiting Mary Lucille one afternoon in May, noticed a spinning wheel sitting in the sewing room and asked if she made her own yarn.

"Well," Mary Lucille told her confidentially, "most of the time I buy it in Fort Wayne when Emmett and I go shopping. But I'm trying something new! It's to be a surprise. I'm hoping to enter something very special this year in the craft fair."

So the word was soon around the circle that Mary Lucille was making something "from scratch," spinning the yarn herself.

"I wonder if she's raising sheep on the side," smirked Loretta Goings.

"Maybe it isn't sheep's wool," Paula Wright said. "Maybe it's from llamas. There are several llamas around."

"I saw alpacas on that farm north of Cranfield where they always have exotic animals," Emojean Billings offered. "Maybe that's where she's getting the wool."

"Well," Mrs. Devington said, "maybe she'll win a prize this year. I know it would do her a lot of good." Mrs. Devington always tried to put the best face on a thing, no matter how poor or unlikely it seemed.

The craft fair opened on Friday noon of the second week in August, during some of the hottest days of the year, "the dog days," Mrs. Goings called them. She said it was because dogs suffer most in the heat of summer.

"Doesn't it have something to do with a star?" Paula Wright asked. "Isn't there a dog star this time of year?"

"I don't know anything about that," Mrs. Goings said. "I just know our old dog Trooper suffers with the heat."

The local folks obligingly showed up, browsing the wares exhibited in the community building at Bennett's Park, and eating hot dogs or hamburgers prepared by the Thornburg Lions Club. The Boy Scouts sold lemonade and the Baptist Men's Fellowship made homemade ice cream to supplement these delicacies.

The general consensus, as folks entered the building and gazed at the hung-up quilts, was one of amazement at their intricate designs and careful craftsmanship. The tables of knitted garments and needlework were equally praised, but they were all so impressive that nothing stood out as unquestionably superior. The ladies had begun around eight o'clock that morning arranging the room and directing their husbands in hanging the quilts on frames they had built at home. Throughout the morning the entries were registered and placed as the women brought them. By noon most of the quilts were hung and the tables nearly filled with the smaller items.

Mrs. Devington and her committee had just sat down in the shade of a maple tree to eat lunch when one of them said, "I haven't seen Mary Lucille yet today. Isn't she coming?"

"I think so," Melvia Markham said. "She's been counting on it so, I'm sure she'll be here."

As she was speaking, Mary Lucille Poteet was seen coming through the park toward the community building, carrying a shopping bag—not by the handles, but in her arms, as if it were a child.

"There she is now," said Mrs. Devington, and stood to welcome her.

"Mary, Dear, we're so glad to see you! Just bring that on inside, and Clara will help you get it registered and placed." She followed Mary Lucille into the building.

"Just fill in this page," Clara said to her, "and be sure to write on the first line what it is that you're entering, and its material contents."

Mary Lucille wrote "Sweater" on the first line, and left blank the space marked "materials." She handed the paper back to Clara and turned to Mrs. Devington.

"Where shall I put it?"

"Well, let's put it here in this space, by Darla Corman's entry," Mrs. Devington said. As Mary Lucille opened the shopping bag and unwrapped its contents, Mrs. Devington gasped.

"Oh, Mary! That's lovely!"

Mary Lucille laid on the table a hand-knit sweater made of homespun yarn, so soft and delicate that Mrs. Devington was hesitant to touch it. Its pastel earth colors blended together like the colors of an autumn sunset. Mary Lucille had chosen pearl buttons for the front, with tinier ones on the sleeve. The collar was ample and lay softly against the shoulders. It was exquisite, making the entries around it look pale by comparison.

"What is it—what did you, uh, make it of?" Mrs. Devington asked.

"I'm afraid that will have to be a secret," Mary Lucille said with a smile, and she went outside to eat some lunch.

Throughout the afternoon and evening, as people strolled through the display, many compliments were paid to the ladies' work, but nothing drew so much comment as Mrs. Poteet's sweater. It was at first thought to be alpaca, because of the alpaca farm north of Cranfield. Then someone ventured a guess at angora. Mrs. Billings drew her reading glasses from her purse and perused the material closely. Then straightening up triumphantly she announced to the ladies gathered around her, "I've seen this before, in a display of exotic materials in Chicago. It's called vicuña."

"What on earth is that?" Paula Wright asked.

"It's a small animal, like a sheep or something, and it lives in South America. Its wool is very expensive." Mrs. Billings lowered her head and shook it as though it might be beyond the means of someone so lowly as Mary Lucille Poteet.

The others gathered around the table more closely and examined the sweater in turn, each venturing a guess at its material. They touched it gingerly, and each said the same thing: "It sure is soft!"

"But where would Mary Lucille get vicuña wool around here? I've never seen it in any of the stores–in Fort Wayne *or* Indianapolis."

"Maybe she sent away for it."

"Emmett Poteet doesn't make that kind of money running a dry cleaning business!" Mrs. Billings assured them. "Someone must have sent it to her."

They touched it once again, then withdrew to find Mary Lucille under the tree, eating a hamburger and drinking lemonade.

"Mary, Dear, your sweater is absolutely beautiful!" gushed Mrs. Billings. "But won't you tell us what it's made of?"

"Nope," was all Mary Lucille would say, and she smiled broadly.

The women indulged her for the moment, but they had no intention of giving up.

"I'll ask my mother when she comes this evening," Paula said. "She'll know. She's knitted just about everything that can be spun into yarn, I think."

That evening and all the next morning, folks tried to guess the material from which Mary Lucille had crafted so beautiful a sweater. Paula's mother said she had no idea what it was. And Mary Lucille wasn't telling.

At four o'clock the auction began. Several quilts brought more than three hundred dollars. A lady from Ohio bought four of them. She had been to previous craft fairs in Thornburg. It was known that she owned a shop somewhere near Columbus and got "horrendous prices" for them, as Mrs. Billings said. Several of the sweater-and-scarf sets went for seventy-five or eighty dollars. At length Mary Lucille's sweater was held up, and a lady from Michigan, a Mrs. Harrison, called out, "One hundred dollars."

The group around the auctioneer inhaled sharply. Paula Wright's mother bid "One hundred twenty-five."

A lady standing next to Mrs. Harrison asked her, "Do you know what it's made of?"

Mrs. Harrison simply bid, "One hundred fifty."

"Mother, what's it made of?" Paula asked.

"Vicuña wool," her mother whispered. "Your Mrs. Billings told me. That stuff is priceless."

The auctioneer was asking for one hundred seventy-five, and Paula's mother raised her hand.

The bidding went on like this until the two women had run the price up to four hundred and fifty dollars.

"That's too rich for me," Paula's mother said, and the sweater went to Mrs. Harrison from Michigan.

As she claimed her prize, the auctioneer said, "Excuse me, Mrs. Harrison, but none of us here have been able to figure out what kind of material the sweater is made of. The lady who made it says it's a secret. Can you tell us?"

The group looked quickly at Mary Lucille, then at Mrs. Harrison, who said clearly and proudly that it was made of the rarest wool in the world, the inner hair of the vicuña, a member of the camel family, and that it lives at high altitudes in the Andes mountains of South America.

"It's *very* expensive wool," she said, "and I'm both delighted and surprised to find it here in Thornburg."

The entire Quilting and Knitting Circle turned to look with astonishment at Mary Lucille.

"Didn't I tell you?" Mrs. Billings said, nudging the woman beside her.

"But where would she *get* wool like that?"

"Heaven only knows," said Mrs. Billings.

Mrs. Harrison paid for the sweater at the cashier's table and left with her purchase.

The Thornburg Women's Quilting and Knitting Circle gathered around Mary Lucille and congratulated her on her accomplishment, and Mary Lucille beamed with pride.

The next morning in church, Melvia Markham sat down in the pew beside Mary Lucille. The organ prelude covered their voices as Melvia said quietly,

"Now that the fair is over, can you tell us what the material was from which you made the sweater?"

Mary Lucille smirked at her bulletin, then she looked up and said, "You have to promise never to tell anyone."

Melvia thought a moment then said, "All right, I won't. It'll be our secret."

"I made the yarn from dryer lint after I dried Emmett's nightshirts," she whispered.

Melvia's mouth dropped open, then she laughed quietly to herself and shook her head.

"Are you serious?"

"Absolutely! I always thought it should be good for something. Now I've contributed four hundred and fifty dollars to the scholarship fund."

And she smiled the smile of one who had at last been taken into the inner circle.

After the Battle

Robert James Pitman was honorably discharged from the United States Army on September 1, 1953. By the following Monday he was on a troop ship heading out of Kanghwa Bay, Korea, into the Yellow Sea, bound for America. After rounding the southern coast of Japan, the ship stopped at the Hawaiian Islands. Two weeks later it sailed for San Diego and home. By October, most of the men had mustered out and were on trains and planes for their home states. Robert was focused on Thornburg, Indiana.

He called his folks from San Diego to tell them he was stateside and would soon be home. His plane arrived in Indianapolis the next morning, and he called again. He and two other fellows rented a car. He would be home yet that afternoon. He could hear his mother crying for joy on the other end of the phone. His father took the receiver and said, "Son, is it really you?"

"It's really me, Pop. I'm nearly home." His voice broke once, then he said, "I should be there for supper."

"Hold on, Son, Mom wants to talk to you."

"What do you want for supper, Robert?" his mother asked in a quavering voice.

"Anything, as long as it isn't kimchi," he said. "Anything will be fine. I just want to get home."

"I understand, Honey. We'll have supper waiting. Just be careful driving. We love you!"

"I love you too," Robert said. "See you soon." He hung up the phone.

To have him so close to home brought his mother nearly to collapse. He'd been gone three years. His letters had been filled with depressing references to battles, the men in his company, his health, the Korean countryside, and how much he missed home. He had not mentioned Carolyn Amick, the girl he had left behind.

David Claremont had been very attentive to Carolyn since Robert's departure, and Carolyn had to admit to herself that she enjoyed the attention. David was good looking and available, employed by the Farm Co-op. Once or twice he had shown up at parties where Carolyn was and offered to take her home. She accepted the first time, then declined thereafter.

"Robert and I are practically engaged; it wouldn't seem right."

But David persisted, calling her on weekends for movie dates or "just a walk." She kept refusing him, but it had become more difficult as letters from Robert seemed fewer and farther between. His writing sounded strained; she wondered if he was having second thoughts about their relationship.

Maybe he had fallen in love with a Korean girl! Maybe the war had changed him so much that he couldn't love her anymore. Maybe . . . . She stopped herself from that line of thinking and tried to focus on her work as a kindergarten teacher.

But as the months became years, David Claremont became a comforting presence. She had at last accepted his invitation to a movie, then to a picnic—just the two of them along Bode's Creek under a weeping willow tree. The grass there was long and lush; they had spread a blanket and eaten their lunch. David had helped her repack the basket, then put his arms around her and kissed her.

She had been flustered and confused about her emotions, but it had felt wonderful. Her first kiss in more than a year! She had told him that it couldn't become anything more than friendship, because she was waiting for Robert to come home.

"What if he doesn't come home?" David had asked her.

She lay awake that night in tears, conjuring up images of him dead on the battlefield. She got out his letters and read them again, searching for any word that might indicate that he still loved her, that he was hoping to come home and marry her. But they were about everything else, most of which she could not relate to. She had refused the idea that he no longer loved her. They had been so close ever since high school, even when she was away at college before he was drafted. He would drive the hundred or so miles to see her on weekends; she had gradually come to expect that their love would blossom into marriage.

Then, in the early summer of '53, when it seemed the war would last forever, she and David had talked of marriage. She told him she was not in love with him, but she didn't want to be an "old maid" either. Maybe she could learn to love him if Robert didn't return, or if he came back and told her he didn't love her anymore. She tried to be honest with David as well as with herself. The truth was that Robert occupied her thoughts nearly every minute.

Dorothy Pitman called Carolyn immediately after she talked with Robert.

"Our boy's on his way home!" she practically sang into the phone. "He just called from Indianapolis, he'll be here for supper. Why don't you come over too?"

A sudden knot clutched Carolyn in the midriff. It would be too awkward to be sitting at his folks' supper table if Robert didn't want to see her. She declined, saying she wanted to see him alone the first time. His mother understood.

"I'm sure he'll be calling you, Dear," she said. "Bye-bye."

Robert's reunion with his parents was freighted with a mixture of joy and anguish. Supper around the oval oak table brought back memories so poignant that he could hardly eat for the lump in his throat. Other memories kept flashing through his mind, clouding the joy of his homecoming. He left the table once to go into another room and try to clear his head. Coming home was harder than he had imagined.

"Are you all right, Dear?" his mother kept asking. "You don't seem quite like yourself."

"Now, Honey, it just takes some getting used to," Jim told her. "After all, he's jumped half-way around the world in a couple of weeks. Just give him time, right Robert?"

Robert smiled weakly and said he was just tired from traveling.

"Well, a good night's sleep will do wonders for you," his mother said. "I've made up your old room for you. You'll have to excuse the boxes in the closet. I needed some extra storage space. But everything else is the same. I even hung up your graduation picture!"

Robert pushed his chair back from the table and stood up. "Thanks for the great meal, Mom," he said. "It sure tasted good!"

He went into the living room and sat on the sofa, looking around at the familiar things he had not seen in three years. He went out and stood on the porch, breathing in the cool autumn evening. In spite of himself, memories of another kind of air, another landscape, crowded his mind. He heard not the cars on Main Street, but tanks; not screen doors slamming, but guns. He came back in the house and went upstairs. The door to his old room was open; his bed stood in the same place it had always stood. The curtains were the same, and the wallpaper, and the rug by the bed.

"I put out clean towels for you in the bathroom," his mother called up the stairs. "They're the blue ones. Is there anything else you need?"

A space of silence intervened before he said, "No. No, Mom. It's, uh, just fine. Thanks."

He sat on the bed and stared at the room. So small. So familiar and yet so alien. So empty. Emotions he had tried to suppress for three years welled up in him, and he turned face down on the bed and sobbed, clawing at the covers.

After a while, Jim Pitman went upstairs to see if his son was all right. He found him asleep on the bed, face down, still in his clothes. Jim stood and looked at him a long minute, then went back downstairs.

"I think he's just worn out," he said to his wife. "Let's just let him sleep in the morning as long as he wants to."

"I just wish he'd talk to us," Dorothy said. "He's so quiet! It worries me."

"I know," Jim replied, "but I think it's often that way with guys who come home from the war. The adjustment must be pretty hard. We'll just give him time. He'll come around."

By ten o'clock the next morning, Robert still had not come downstairs. His mother went up to see if he was sleeping. She heard him in the bathroom taking a shower, so she looked in his room to see if he needed anything. He had not slept under the covers, that was obvious. And the picture of Carolyn she had put on the night stand was missing. She went back downstairs and busied herself with household chores, mostly to occupy her mind. Robert's behavior worried her exceedingly.

When he finally came down, he was dressed in blue jeans and a pullover sweater, with white athletic socks on his feet. He went to the back door and looked out at the yard. Then he pulled out a kitchen chair from the table and sat down, yawning once.

Dorothy came into the kitchen and said a little too brightly, "Well! Good morning! Are you hungry? You sure slept long enough to be!"

"Just coffee, Mom," he answered. He looked as tired as when he went to bed.

"Are you sure you don't want some cinnamon rolls? They're fresh from the bakery this morning. Your father made a special trip uptown to get them."

"No, just coffee." His voice was a monotone.

She poured his coffee and sat down opposite him, studying his face. He had aged years since he left home. How could three years put so much wear on a young man! His eyes were not in the same room with his body, but seemed to see things a thousand miles away. Ten thousand! Jim was right; it would take time. It would be hard for them all, letting him find his own pace, coming home in his own way. She wondered if Carolyn could understand the change in him.

After a while she asked, "What would you like to do today?"

He looked up at her as if that were the stupidest question in the world, said nothing, and finished his coffee. As he set his cup down he said quietly, "Not much, I guess."

He got up and went back upstairs, put on his jacket and a pair of loafers, and came down to the front door.

"Think I'll go for a walk," he said, and left the house.

Dorothy dialed Carolyn Amick's number.

"Carolyn, this is Dorothy. I just wondered if Robert had called you yet."

"No. How is he?"

"Uh, he seems OK, but awfully quiet. Jim says it's often that way with boys returning from service, that we just need to give him time."

"I'd like to see him," Carolyn said. "The last letter I had from him was in June. I haven't known what to think. It's like he's forgotten me."

"Well, Dear, I know he's been through some rough times—his letters to us indicated that—and I'm sure I don't understand what it must have been like. I just think we need to be patient with him and . . . ."

"I've been as patient as I know how to be," Carolyn interrupted. "I've had exactly ten letters from him in three years, and there was nothing in them that gave me much hope. I don't know what to think. We can't just pick up where we left off. Too much time has passed. You know what I mean?"

"I know, Honey. It's been hard for all of us. That's the worst part of war. The folks back home can't understand what they've been through. We don't know what to do when they come back, how to help them."

"Well, it may not be the worst part," Carolyn said, "but it sure is hard just sitting at home waiting. I just hope he wants to see me. Would you let me know if there's anything I can do to, you know, make things better?"

"Of course I will, Dear. Now don't you worry, it'll be all right. It'll just take time."

On Sunday morning in church, Robert sat with his parents. The entire congregation did their best to welcome him, and the pastor mentioned his presence during the announcements. During the pastoral prayer he thanked God for "an end to this horrible conflict, and the safe return of our service men and women." Before the Amen, Robert slipped out of his pew and left the church by a side door. His father thought momentarily of going after him, but decided against it.

"I noticed Robert left church this morning," Melvia Markham said. "Is he all right?" She was standing by her husband as the congregation filed out.

"I think he'll be OK in time," his mother said. "He's been through a lot. They say it just takes time for all that to heal."

"I'm sure it must," Melvia said. "Well, you're all in our prayers, you know."

"Thank you," Dorothy said, and left with eyes brimful of tears.

In the middle of the afternoon, Carolyn called the Pitman home, asking to speak to Robert. Dorothy told her he had gone for a walk, but she might catch up to him by the creek.

"He used to like walking by the creek," she said.

Carolyn thanked her and slipped on a jacket. She walked to the creek where it ran under County Road 100 S, then turned north along its western edge where a path had been worn. She couldn't help reflecting that she and David had walked this same path the day of their picnic. She felt conflicted. She wondered how Robert would greet her if she found him. She even felt a bit foolish for pursuing him. After all, he had not even called to tell her he was home. Maybe he didn't want to see her at all. Maybe she had held out hope for nothing.

She came finally to the soft grassy area where she and David had had their picnic. Just beyond it, sitting on a large stone by the creek, was Robert. She tried to pretend her presence there was a happy accident, but she knew she sounded fake.

"Robert! Is that really you? When did you get home?" She approached him but did not sit down.

He stood. "Hello, Carolyn."

She came closer to him and reached out a hand. He took it, and they looked at each other a moment. Then she said, "I actually heard you were home. I mean, it's all over town, so you can't hide out here." She was trying to be lighthearted.

"I wasn't hiding," he said. "I just need some peace and quiet, time to think."

"I hope I'm not bothering you," she said. "Would you rather be alone?"

"No, it's OK," he said. She sat down on a rock near him.

"I still have the letters you sent me," she began. "All of them. I read them over and over."

She smiled at him, hoping for a smile in return.

He stared at the water running past them as he said, "I guess I didn't write much, did I? I'm sorry, I, uh . . . ."

"It's OK, I understand. I know you had a lot on your mind."

He looked at her. "You were on my mind."

"And you were on mine," she answered softly. "Almost all the time."

She struggled for something more to say but thought the silence better.

At last he said, "Are you still, uh, y'know, single?"

"Of course I'm single, Silly," she said, and regretted the word "Silly." "I've been waiting three years for you to come home, praying every night and day that you'd be all right. Weeks went by without any word from you, and I . . . ."

She stopped herself. Her emotions were getting out of hand. She so wanted to be part of the peace he sought, a solid point of reference in his scrambled world. After a space she said,

"Robert, I still love you! I've loved you since high school, and all through college and while you were overseas. I've never stopped loving you. I just want to know if you still love me, if we still have what we used to have."

He stood up and turned away, looking across the fields beyond them. She sat helplessly, wondering if she should leave or stay. She decided she had nothing to lose by letting him know how she felt. She stood and came to him, putting her arm around his waist, laying her head on his shoulder.

He made no move away from her, but he said nothing. His eyes were closed, and he seemed to tremble. She held him this way for a minute or more, then she walked a few steps away and turned to him.

"I'll go now, and let you do what you need to do. Please let me know how I can be helpful."

He said nothing, and she left the way she had come.

By more than coincidence, David Claremont met her on Main Street and asked her how Robert seemed.

"Kinda confused, I think," she replied. "The war really took a toll of him!"

"You think he's the same guy who left you three years ago?"

"He's still Robert," she said, "and I still love him." She looked frankly at David and added, "It'll take time, but we'll be OK."

"I'm still here," David said. "Let me know if you need anything."

She left him standing by the fountain and walked to her house alone.

During the next week the Pitmans got little sleep. Robert would cry out in the night, and they would come to his room to find him sitting up on the edge of his bed, his face a mask of terror. They would sit beside him, their arms around him, until he was calm again. He had had a dream, he said, that was all. This happened several times.

"Honey, I think it might help you to talk with someone about these things," his mother said one morning at breakfast.

"You mean a shrink?"

"I mean someone who understands better than your Dad and I. We've never been through what you've been through, and I just think . . . ."

"I don't want to talk to any headshrinker," he said. "I just need time to get over it all. Can't you understand that?" He left the table and went to his room and slammed the door.

Dorothy sat crying at the table while Jim tried to comfort her. "It just takes time," he said again. But his own worries persisted.

Later that morning he stopped in at Marshal Bates's office.

"Ted, weren't you in the military once?" he asked.

"Just a reserve unit," Ted said. "I never went overseas. All my training was police work. That's different from the infantry."

"I just wonder who Robert could talk to, he seems so lost," his father said.

"Have you suggested a psychiatrist?" Ted asked.

"He won't hear to it," Jim answered. "He had some rest in Hawaii, but he isn't getting over it. He yells out in his sleep nearly every night, and he won't talk to us much. Carolyn said she couldn't get much out of him, either."

"Well, Jim, the best I can offer is to keep an eye on him, be sure he doesn't hurt himself. Let me know if you think of anything else."

Jim thanked him and left. He went next door to the Town Hall, where he was the accountant, and tried to focus his mind on his work.

Dorothy, cleaning the house for the third time that week, tried to forget her son's anguish, but everything she touched reminded her of his troubled homecoming. She found Carolyn's picture face down in his top dresser drawer, and his army things—papers, pictures, souvenir canned rations, a New Testament with a steel cover, an empty machine gun shell—tucked away in a corner of the bottom drawer. She felt guilty about snooping in his things, but she hoped to find something that might give a clue to his depression and perhaps its cure.

On Friday morning, while Robert was out of town for the day with an old high school buddy, she went to Pastor Markham.

"Pastor, I'm so worried about Robert! He's just not himself since he's been home. I don't know what to do for him. We try to give him time and space to get his thoughts straightened out, but nothing seems to help."

"I'd guess that has to feel pretty helpless, being his folks, loving him, and not able to get through to him," Markham said. "And you've suggested that he get help from a professional?"

"Yes. He won't listen to it. He just walks away." She sat and looked at the floor a minute. "Do you think he'd talk to you?"

"You might ask him," the pastor replied. "He seemed cordial enough last Sunday when he came to church, but then I noticed he left early."

"I'll ask him if he'd feel comfortable talking with you," Dorothy said. "If you think of anything Jim and I can do to help him, please let us know."

He assured her that he would, and she left.

At home that evening, Robert seemed to be better. His trip to Indianapolis with his old school buddy, Marty, had been fun, he said. They had talked about old times. They went to a movie but left halfway through it and sat in a bar drinking beer for a while. Marty talked about his two years in a community college, then his work as an appliance repairman. He had not asked about Robert's experiences in Korea, and Robert had not volunteered any information. It seemed good to forget it for a while, to pretend that the three years had not intervened.

But in the middle of the night Jim and Dorothy were awakened suddenly by cries from Robert's room. Going in, they found him sobbing into his pillow, saying over and over, "I'm sorry, I'm sorry, I'm sorry."

Dorothy sat by her son and held him. He laid his head against her and cried until he was exhausted and went back to sleep. She and Jim lay in their bed and talked until daylight began to show through the window. They got up and started another day.

Robert left the house a little before noon and turned toward Main Street. He had a notion of walking until his mind was cleared of all its demons, even if it took all night. He had reached the railroad, intending to walk into the country on 100 S, when David Claremont called to him. David had been hitting baseballs across the park and was retrieving them along Jefferson Street as Robert passed.

"Hey, Buddy, welcome home!" he called.

Robert turned and stopped. "Thanks," he said.

"So, how's it seem, being back on home soil?"

"Pretty good, I guess." He and David had been classmates in high school, but never close.

"I saw Carolyn yesterday; she said you were home."

"That right?"

"I've tried to keep the wolves away from her while you were gone. She's a great gal!"

"Yeah, she sure is," Robert said. His voice lacked any emotion at all.

"So, you guys getting married now?" David pursued.

"We, uh, haven't had time to talk about it," Robert said. "I'll see you later."

He turned and walked on into the country, wondering just what David meant by "keeping the wolves away from her." What had transpired in the years he was away? Who were the "wolves," anyway? And did Carolyn really love him as much as she professed? Was he a fool for thinking she would wait for him? And who appointed David Claremont her protector? Robert was beginning to feel anger toward both of them. Was he only humiliating himself by coming home to Thornburg? Would he have been better off staying in San Diego, finding a job there?

Saturday the weather was brisk. Clouds covered the sun, and a cold wind blew through the town. A light mist dampened Robert's jacket as he trudged east on Jefferson Street, past the last of the houses. He turned into the field where the water tower stood and slogged through the grass to its base. An iron ladder ascended its side; he began to climb. The tower was old and needed paint. An iron grating around its tank served as a walkway for repairmen. He climbed onto it and stood at its railing, looking far away, beyond the town, toward the west, toward Korea. His face was like stone.

A single figure had followed him out of town, watched as he climbed the ladder, and now stood in the grass some seventy-five feet below him. He looked down at Carolyn Amick, who looked up at him with tears running down her face.

He called down to her, "What are you doing here?"

"Robert, I want to talk to you."

"There's nothing to say. You should go home now."

"I'm not going home until you come down."

He walked to the other side of the tower. She followed on the ground, looking up at him, praying that he would not jump.

"Robert, I love you! I want you to come down. Please!"

He did not reply.

"Then I'm coming up."

"No!" he shouted down to her. "Go home!"

She made no reply, but started to climb the ladder. She began to get dizzy on the tenth rung, and hesitated. He was watching her from the walkway and called down,

"You can't come up here, it's too dangerous. Anyway, you're afraid of heights, remember? You'll never make it. Go on home!"

His memory that she was afraid of heights touched her. He remembered that small fact about her! Maybe she had not been completely expunged from his thoughts those three years! Maybe he knew her better than she thought. She took another step on the ladder, then another, not looking down but only up at Robert. Her hands were white as she gripped the cold iron of the ladder. Her love drove her on, beyond the limits of her fear, with only the object of her love in mind: to comfort Robert and assure him that no matter what he had been through, he was still the man she loved, that life could go on.

When she was near the top, Robert extended his hand and pulled her up, and she stood beside him on the walkway. The wind blew stronger here. She leaned against the tower and breathed hard, trying to steady her nerves. Robert still held her hand.

"You shouldn't have come up here. I'm not worth the risk."

Tears filled her eyes as she touched his face and said, "You're worth a lot more than this."

He sat down on the walkway, his back against the tower, and stared out over the fields beyond the town.

"You don't know me," he said quietly. He was trembling. She put her arm around his shoulders and drew him close.

"Then tell me who you are," she said. "I want to know you. I want to know everything that's happened to you."

"No you don't," he said. "Oh God! Things have happened to me that no one should know."

"I don't think love hides from anything," she said. "I think love is able to take whatever comes, no matter how hard it is. And I do love you, more than you know."

They sat in silence a few minutes as the wind blew across their tear-stained faces. She turned up her collar, then his.

"I saw David Claremont today," he said. "He says he's been looking after you while I was gone. What did he mean by that?"

"Robert, David and I are just friends. We went to a movie once or twice, and we've talked some, but that's about it. I could never be serious about anyone but you."

He was quiet a long time. At length he said,

"Carolyn, I'm so afraid! I'm afraid that the man I've become is someone nobody could ever love—not once they knew me."

"You have to take that risk," she said. "You can't get past whatever it is that's tearing you up until you do. Please, just trust my love enough to tell me who you've become."

He sat silent and motionless for several minutes. She rubbed his hand to keep it warm.

"I didn't write much to you," he said presently, "because the things I had experienced were too terrible to put on paper. I couldn't send that home."

He turned his face to hers and said, "I've done things that I never thought I would do. Horrible things that no one should have to do."

He looked down at the ground far below them. The wind at this height was stronger and colder than it was on the ground. It seemed right to him that he should suffer its bite and feel its chill in his bones.

"I've killed people. Not just one. Lots of them."

She pulled him closer to her and held him as he cried, and she cried with him.

"It's over now, Sweetheart," she said, trembling. "No matter what you had to do, it's over now. You're home. You're safe."

He pulled violently away from her and stood up, gripping the railing, looking down. "It's not over!" he shouted, as if to announce it to the world. "It'll never be over! I can't bring back those men who died over there, and I can't quit dreaming about it."

He turned to her defiantly and said amid sobs, "You can't understand, you weren't there!"

She answered him steadily, still sitting against the tower, trying to hold her emotions in check.

"I can understand that a good man suffers when he has to do things he's ordered to do that are against his conscience. And I know that you are a good man, no matter what happened over there."

"Carolyn," he began, kneeling on the grating beside her, "I could never have believed that I would do what I did, until I was doing it. But I didn't have any choice. We were at Finger Hill—that's north of the 38th parallel, in communist country—and we were dug in. The enemy just kept coming over the hill, and we just kept shooting them. They wouldn't stop coming! The bodies kept piling up until they could hardly climb over them. And they still kept coming!"

He broke down and cried again. She pulled his head to her shoulder and put her arms around him.

"I can't believe it even now," he sobbed. "We had a machine gun and enough ammo to last as long as they kept coming. It got to be a stupid game! Some of the guys were laughing at the sheer idiocy of it. A bunch of Gooks that didn't have enough sense to quit running into our bullets! It was sickening, and yet we couldn't stop. We knew if they got through, we'd all be dead. It was either them or us, and we had the advantage. They never quit 'til it was too dark to see."

He turned his tear-streaked face to hers. "How can anyone love somebody who does things like that?"

"Oh Sweetheart!" she cried, "love isn't for perfect people. It's for people like you and me who do the only things we know. None of us are perfect. War is terrible. The people who have to go and fight do what they have to do to survive. Sure it's horrible, but that doesn't make you a horrible person."

"Why can't I forget it!" he cried. "Why do I still feel I have to go back and make it right? And I know I can't!"

"Only God can make things right on this earth," she said. "All we can do is what we know, and we don't really know very much. We make mistakes every day. I know I do. Sometimes we do things we wish we could take back, and can't. That's why God's love is our only hope. He wraps it around us and loves us in every terrible moment of our lives, when we're lost and wandering and doing things we know we don't want to do, just because we feel desperate. If we can't trust Him to love us in those times, then love doesn't mean very much."

He looked into her eyes for the first time. He seemed to be searching her soul for a truth that would not desert him. In her honest gaze he quieted.

"You believe that, don't you," he said simply. It wasn't so much a question as a discovery. She held him close and rocked him gently.

"It's all I have to go on. I prayed for you every day you were away, because I couldn't be there to protect you. But I knew God could, that no matter what you faced, His love would see you through it. I know that now, right now, sitting up here on this water tower, He forgives everything you've done that's tearing at your soul. God isn't looking back at your past, Honey, He's looking forward at your future."

He raised his head from her shoulder and looked at her again.

"What future do I have?" he asked.

"Robert James Pitman, I love you. I want to marry you and love you for the rest of my life."

Her face was as calm as a summer day. The sincerity and fearlessness in it were the picture of home to Robert. He smiled at her through his tears for the first time, and gently she kissed him.

"Let's go down and get some lunch," she said.

They sat in silence a while longer, then he stood.

"OK," he said. He took her hand and lifted her up.

He went first down the ladder, to help steady her, but she climbed down without fear, joy and hope strengthening her for every step. They walked hand in hand back into town and into a future that had no guarantees but the ineffable and certain love of God.

Them Japs

"What this town needs is jobs," George McAbee declared. "We need a major corporation moving in here. I don't care what they do as long as they provide jobs for our people."

The Town Council sat in silence until its president, Betty Allison, spoke. "Well, we certainly need jobs, but I think we do care what kind of corporation it would be."

"Well, you know what I mean: any decent outfit that could provide employment for our working force," George said. "We've got eighteen hundred people in this town, and about two hundred of us are out of work. When the canning factory left, there wasn't anything to take its place. Now we've got folks driving to Indianapolis, Fort Wayne, even Dayton, Ohio, just to make a living. We gotta get a business in here."

"Our county Economic Development Committee is working on it," Betty replied. She had had to deal with this problem every council meeting for the past year, and they were making no headway on it. "They have some leads, I hear, but nothing definite yet."

"What leads?" Dave Scarborough asked.

"Well, don't quote me on this, but I think a Japanese company is interested. I believe they do something with electronics." Betty was not being purposefully vague; she simply had little information.

The Economic Development Committee had been dragging its feet. Most of the applicants for real estate on which to build a company had poor backing by investors and often an undesirable product. A meat packing plant had applied, but the town thought that would create a bad odor. A landfill had been proposed and turned down. A large hog farming operation on the edge of town was likewise rejected. One or two small companies hiring twenty to thirty employees did not seem to be the answer, and they were referred to other communities.

Darrell Baird, one of several veterans in town, stood up.

"Look, I don't want to sound prejudiced, but we don't need a bunch o' them Japs runnin' a company in this town. I saw enough of them in the war. They don't have the morals we have. We don't want them around here. Their kids would be going to our schools, playin' with our kids on the playground. In ten years they'd be datin' our kids. First thing you know, some of 'em would get married, and then you got little half-breeds runnin' around. It'd ruin the town!"

Paul Hartman was the high school social studies teacher, and when he talked, folks generally listened. He was soft-spoken but direct, obviously knowledgeable and not given to panic.

"Well, Darrell, those of us who were too young to go to that war can hardly have your perspective. And yet I think it might be pointed out that we're all 'half-breeds,' even 'quarter-breeds,' and more complex breeds than that."

Darrell scoffed, "I ain't no half-breed!"

"Well, your father's people descended from the Scots, but your mother was a Mueller," Hartman pointed out. "Her folks immigrated from Germany. Dave here came from English stock on his father's side, but his mother was French. My own family is a mixture of German, English, and Irish, with a Swede or two thrown in for good measure. Most of the families in town are mixed nationalities. We came here from a dozen countries or more. I think we forget that the only native Americans were the folks our ancestors ran off the land and put on reservations. Julia Nighthawk up at Conger is the only unmixed breed in the area that I know. Her ancestors lived here for thousands of years before ours came.

"So I think the argument that a company owned by another nationality would corrupt us doesn't really hold water. From the native Americans' point of view, we were the ones who did the corrupting."

"Well, I'm just an old farmer, but I know what I saw," Darrell said. "And I know that us Germans and English and whatnot have built a better country than the Indians ever had, and I don't intend to give it up. We've fought hard for what we've got, and it's worth protecting. All I'm sayin' is, let's not hand it over to a bunch of orientals who don't understand our ways. They'll likely try to change everything we hold dear and sacred. They ain't Christian, for one thing, and that makes a big difference."

"I suppose it depends on which orientals we're talking about," Paul replied. "Some Japanese *are* Christians, and many of them have a higher standard of living than some of our local folks. I don't think we ought to reject them out of hand, simply because of their nationality."

Several opinions were voiced, most of them at once, so that nothing was heard clearly. Betty rapped her gavel to restore order and said, "I think we need to move along to some other issues on the agenda."

After the meeting, Darrell and a couple of others stood outside the town hall and rehashed the Second World War and the Japanese atrocities they had witnessed. Sharing their stories, they bolstered their prejudice against orientals in general and the Japanese in particular, and went home more strongly convinced than ever that Japan had no business in Thornburg.

Several weeks later the chairperson of the Economic Development Committee got a call from the president of a Japanese electronics company. He wanted to bring a group to Thornburg to look at the possibilities for business in the area. He spoke fluent English and was very courteous. The chairperson extended an invitation, they agreed on a date, and the news was forwarded to the local newspaper.

When the article appeared the following week, stating that a group of Japanese businessmen was coming to Thornburg, it was the talk of the town. Betty's telephone was busy into the late hours of the evening. Gossip spread like a grass fire that Arlie Placer's farm had already been sold to the Japanese, and Arlie and his wife were retiring to Florida with their wealth.

When Darrell Baird heard that, he drove out to Arlie's farm north of town. "Arlie, what in Sam Hill do you mean, sellin' your place to them Japs!" Darrell demanded to know.

"Now hold on a minute, Darrell," Arlie said. "First place, I didn't sell my farm to nobody, and I ain't a' goin' to."

"Well, all's I know is, a couple guys come over yesterday and was sayin' you was gonna sell your farm to 'em, so I just wondered."

"Well, you just put your mind at ease on that score, 'cause we ain't movin' anyplace. I was born and raised on this farm, and I intend to die here."

Then his demeanor changed and his voice became conspiratorial as he said, "But the fact is, they're gonna build somewhere around here, you can bet on that. And they'll likely bring a bunch of them Japs with 'em. Our people won't have any more jobs than they got right now."

"Well, I for one aim to do everything I can to stop it," Darrell vowed. "That Economic Development bunch can say what they like, but it won't do our community any good to have a bunch of shovelheads over here meddlin' in our business."

"What d'ya aim to do?" Arlie asked.

"Well, I'm gonna start with a petition, see how many names I can get on it, and present it to the Economic Development Committee. If that don't stop it, I think our Town Council ought to pass a law that no foreigners can do business within twenty miles of Thornburg."

"I don't think the Council has that kind of authority," Arlie said. "But maybe they could make a statement sayin' we oppose foreign companies in the area."

"That won't do no good," Darrell persisted. "You gotta have somethin' with teeth in it. I think a bunch of us ought to show up at the Development Council and just tell 'em we won't stand still for it. You with me?"

Arlie looked across his newly planted cornfield and thought a moment, then said, "Tell you what: let's start with the petition and go from there. Maybe the Town Council could take the petition to the Development Committee. That'd let 'em know how we feel. I don't think a bunch of us goin' into the Committee meeting'll do anything but make trouble. We need to go about this in the right way. Let's try the petition first."

In the two weeks preceding the June meeting of the Town Council, Darrell Baird circulated a petition which stated: "We the undersigned reject the notion of any foreign companies doing business in or near the town of Thornburg, Indiana." He got several like-minded citizens to help distribute it, and by the time of the Council meeting, there were one hundred and thirty-one names on it, along with addresses and telephone numbers. He came to the meeting armed with the petition, a sheaf of pages bearing the names of descendents from at least ten foreign countries.

After the Pledge of Allegiance to the flag, Betty opened the meeting with a rap of the gavel and asked for the minutes of the previous meeting. The treasurer's report followed, then she opened the floor for "new business." Darrell got to his feet and cleared his throat.

"Madam chairman and fellow members of the council, I'd like to present this petition which was circulated among our town folks in the last few weeks. If it's OK, I'll just read the opening line. There's a hundred and thirty-one names on it."

"All right, Darrell, go ahead," Betty said.

Darrell read the statement at the top of the petition, following it with, "All the names on these pages are folks that believe as I do that foreign companies have no business in our town. I move that the Council accept this petition and send it to the Economic Development Committee."

Several voices seconded the motion—dozens of citizens had come to the meeting to argue the issue—and it was properly before the body. More than forty-five minutes of discussion ensued, some of it heated, and at last the vote was taken. It passed by a simple majority, and the victorious supporters left the meeting, not caring about the other agenda. Their issue was now before the Economic Development Committee. They were hopeful that foreign intervention in their community had been averted.

When the petition came before the Economic Development Committee, the members were stunned into silence. At length one of the members asked, "Aren't they the town that was asking for a corporation last year? I thought they were in dire need of jobs over there."

"Well, it seems they don't want any foreign companies in their town," the chairman responded. "But the fact is, most American companies of the size they're talking about go to the large cities: GE, Harvester, Ford, all of 'em. I wonder what their beef is about foreign companies?"

"They're afraid foreigners will own their land and eventually take over the town," one of the members said. "I talked with this Mr. Baird who started the petition. I've known him for years. He's dead set against 'em. Especially the Japanese."

"What about a German company, then, or one from England?" someone suggested.

"They'd probably have a better chance," the chairman said, "though I don't know about the Germans. Maybe they'd have the same trouble here."

"You know, I think what they need is to talk with someone from a Japanese company and see what kind of people they are," said a woman on the committee. "Maybe if they got to know them, they'd get over this fear of foreigners. Our daughter spent six months in Kyoto as an exchange student last year. We had a lovely Japanese girl in our home during that time. We never had any trouble with her, and she spoke English almost as good as we do. I think we ought to invite one of these Japanese businesses over here to take a look at us, and let us take a look at them."

"Well, if they come, Thornburg had better agree to let them look around," the chairman said. "I'll contact Mrs. Allison over there and see if it can be arranged. But I think we're in for some conflict."

"It's worth a try," one member said. "I move we invite them to come."

This was seconded and passed, and a letter of invitation was issued to the Japanese company that had shown an interest in establishing its electronics division in America. In less than two weeks, the chairman of the Economic Development Committee had a letter of acceptance from a Mr. Tsukamoto in Yokohama, proposing to arrive in thirty days to look for a suitable location. The Committee chairman called him to confirm the date, and it was announced to the Thornburg Town Council.

The Japanese group arrived by limousine from the Weir-Cook Indianapolis airport on a Tuesday of the following month. They were accompanied by three members of the Economic Development Committee who had driven there to meet them. The group toured the town, driving past the school, the businesses on Main Street, and the residential parts of town. Thornburgers stood unabashedly along the curbs and gawked at them in silence. Darrell Baird stood on Main Street in front of the bank, vigorously waving an American flag as the vehicle passed.

The visitors drove out to the piece of the interstate that had been completed as far as the county seat. Arlie Placer followed at a distance in his '51 Plymouth, eager for any sign of the property the foreigners might be considering. When the limousine turned toward the county seat, Arlie went home.

The evening paper later that month reported that Nippon America intended to build a four million dollar structure just north of Thornburg, Indiana, employing 240 workers. The town was electrified. Betty's phone was seldom quiet all the next day. Just which property were they considering? The Woodson farm? The Brandeis place? Grover Steel's woods? What would it do to the sewage system in town? What about the drain on the electrical system? Alarm was the general mood: the Japanese would move into town and change the face of it forever.

All sorts of horrors were supposed, from the loss of property values to the requirement that all students in school learn Japanese. John Abbot was concerned about the availability of Japanese foods. Clara Morgan, the librarian, wondered if she could find Japanese literature to stock the shelves.

"I read somewhere that they carry those long swords with them, concealed in their clothes," one woman said. "Why, a body wouldn't be safe on the streets!"

"I think they all know Judo," said her companion. "Our marshal wouldn't stand a chance against a gang of them."

"And they smell bad," said another, who had inherited a kimono from her grandmother, made of silk and kept in an old trunk for fifty years. "And you can't believe what they eat!"

"Well, the only thing to do is just stay away from 'em," said the first woman. "Maybe if we don't have anything to do with 'em, they'll just go away."

At a Monday morning gathering of the ministers in town, Rev. Corman, president of the ministerium, said that an influx of Asians in this midwestern community would certainly present a challenge. The others, with furrowed brows, agreed. The general imagination was of strange-looking houses sprouting up around town, with strange-looking people living in them eating strange foods, speaking an incomprehensible language, and bringing new dangers to the community with which the educators and law enforcement officials were unprepared to deal. After all, these were descendents of the people we had bombed in the war. Wouldn't they be bent on revenge?

In desperation, Betty Allison went to the school to talk with Paul Hartman. Could he do something to alleviate the anxiety surrounding the coming of the new corporation? Maybe a public lecture or a series of studies about the Japanese? He thought a few moments, then said he would call her in a day or two.

On Wednesday morning he called, suggesting that he might meet with concerned citizens on Tuesday evenings at the library to talk about Japanese culture and customs, and about their progress since the war.

"A lot has changed since Darrell Baird fought in the South Pacific," he said. "Maybe a little updating on the world situation will help."

"I certainly hope so!" said Betty. "It sure can't hurt anything. The town's all in an uproar. I just hope we can get it calmed down before the Japanese arrive."

The Tuesday evening gathering was announced in the local paper. Eleven citizens showed up besides Paul Hartman. For three weeks, Paul met with the group in the conference room of the library. They were full of questions that betrayed their lack of knowledge about Japan or Asia in general. Paul was obviously informed about the subject. Word got around that the sessions were bringing things to light that most townsfolk had never heard. Others joined the group in the following weeks.

By the fourth session the discussions had to be moved to the high school auditorium. Before school began in September, more than a hundred were in regular attendance at the Tuesday sessions, much quieter now and eager to hear what Paul was teaching about a culture so far from their own. He had certainly done his homework! He even had slides of Japan to show, and Japanese music on a tape recorder. Near the end of August, he arranged to have a Japanese restaurant in Indianapolis cater a meal for the group. Many were amazed at how good it was.

But Darrell Baird did not attend.

The group had learned how hard Japanese children study, how many hours they put in each day on math, science, social studies, and English language.

"You mean they learn English as a regular part of their studies?" asked Julie Pratt. She was a third grade teacher in Thornburg. "I wonder why we aren't requiring a foreign language of *our* students."

Marie Holdcraft, fourth grade teacher, said, "It seems to me we should find someone to teach us Japanese. At least enough to understand these people when they come."

"Maybe we'd like to ask a representative of their company to visit us," Paul suggested. They agreed that it would be a good idea and asked Paul to pursue it. The next morning he called the chairperson of the Economic Development Committee and asked how to contact Nippon America. The chairperson gave him a phone number there in the county seat and the man's name in English spelling.

"You'll like him, I promise," said the chairperson. "He's a happy guy who's looking forward to the adventure. Make him welcome!"

"I sure will," Paul replied, and he dialed the telephone number. A secretary with a familiar midwestern voice answered and told Paul that Mr. Tsukamoto was out of the office just now, but he would be glad to return the call as soon as he came in. Paul thanked the lady and left his number.

Just after one o'clock Paul's telephone rang. A distinctive oriental voice said in excellent English, "This is Mr. Tsukamoto at Nippon America. I believe you called this morning."

"Yes, thank you!" Paul replied. "I'm a social studies teacher here in Thornburg High School. Several of us have been meeting once a week to talk about Japan, your culture and customs, and what your company might mean to our community. We wonder if you could come talk with us about it."

"I would be most happy to do so," Mr. Tsukamoto said. "We have a public relations person, Miss Kyobe, who would be glad to come with me. When would be most convenient for you?"

They agreed on the next Tuesday evening, and Paul spread the word. In Thornburg that took about forty minutes. The town was both excited and apprehensive about the meeting. Betty's main concern was that Darrell Baird not show up to embarrass them.

On Tuesday evening the auditorium was full. Darrell sat on the back row. People stared openly at the two representatives of Nippon America, who sat on the stage beside Paul Hartman while Betty made some preliminary remarks.

"And we hope"—here she turned to look at the visitors—"that your company will provide lots of new jobs for our town." She left the stage and sat down in the front row of seats, while Paul took the podium and introduced the guests.

"Friends, we've learned a lot in the past few weeks about a country most of us have never seen, about customs that are strange to us, and a language we could hardly pronounce even if we knew the words. In the last week I've talked with Mr. Tsukamoto, the representative of Nippon America. I've found him to be well educated in the English language. Maybe even better than some of us!"

Several folks laughed at this, aware of their own inattention to the rules of English.

"We also learned that they're expecting their work force to come from the surrounding community, not from Japan. The idea is to bring their advanced technology in electronics to the American market, and for that they need American workers, people who already live here. They've gone to great lengths to research our state and local community, and they believe this is the place where they can make the greatest contribution and thrive as a company.

"So now I'm happy to introduce to you the chief representative of Nippon America, Mr. Tsukamoto, and his assistant, Miss Kyobe."

Applause broke out immediately. The audience stood as Mr. Tsukamoto and Miss Kyobe bowed politely. Then Mr. Tsukamoto took the podium.

"Thank you very much for that warm welcome! Please sit down. I'm not used to such applause."

He hesitated a moment while the audience sat down.

"Miss Kyobe and I represent a new adventure in America for our company. We will be followed in the days ahead by others who will construct the actual building. By spring we expect to begin production. We will need two hundred and forty employees to make our company succeed. We hope many of those employees will come from Thornburg."

Enthusiastic applause interrupted him.

Mr. Tsukamoto bowed again and continued, "I do not have a long speech to make. We are happy to be here, and we look forward to making many new friends. Fourteen or fifteen of us will be making Indiana our home in the next year. We hope to learn much from you. And we hope we can share something of our land and people. Thank you for welcoming us so well!"

Paul fielded questions from the audience for the next thirty minutes, and Mr. Tsukamoto answered them. People were curious about the product they would make, the ecological impact on the community, the economic and political considerations, and what the pay scale might look like.

Then Miss Kyobe came to the microphone. She spoke in a sweet, clear voice, greeting them in Japanese, then translating: "Greetings from Japan to our friends in America. We have been looking forward a long time to coming, and we know we will find many good friends here. Thank you!"

The meeting broke up. Several clutches of folks stood in the hall or outside the school and talked about the evening.

"Well, I just hope they're as good as their word," Darrell Baird said. "I never knew one yet you could trust."

Several others standing with him seemed grave, although they had to admit that Mr. Tsukamoto made a good presentation.

"That Miss Kyobe is kinda purty," Arlie said. "I wonder if all them Japanese women are that purty."

When construction of the building began in late September, several folks were regulars at the site, standing at a distance or sitting in their cars on a side road, watching the earthmovers, the huge trucks hauling in steel, the cranes erecting the walls and ceilings. Workers from the county seat and several from Thornburg had hired on to put up the structure. Word got around that the Japanese were pretty good folks to work for.

"Real courteous," one man said. "Nobody yells at you. They just tell you what comes next and expect you to do it. The foreman's a guy I knew from a job over in Ohio. He says he's worked for them Japanese before, and they treat their employees real well."

On Halloween night a pickup with its lights out turned off the highway into the construction area. A tall figure with a hooded sweatshirt over his coveralls crept through the mud to the half-finished building of Nippon America. He carried two sticks of dynamite and a length of fuse. These he put under a corner of the structure and strung the fuse along a row of boards laid down as a walkway. Then he lighted the fuse, got into his truck, and backed out. He drove east out of town and was well away from the construction site when the explosion occurred. It brought down the front corner of the building and with it parts of the first and second floors.

When the crew came to work at dawn, the foreman told everyone to stay in their cars and not make any footprints. Then he drove into town and found Marshal Bates. Together they came back to the construction site and surveyed the damage.

"Well, the only person I can think of to do something like this is Darrell Baird," Ted said.

"He the guy who's been against this from the start?" the foreman asked.

"I'm afraid so," Ted said. "He's carried a grudge against Japan ever since the war, and I guess he hasn't got over it yet."

Ted noted the tire tracks and footprints, then he drove out to Darrell's place. It was a farm east of town with a long lane to the house and barn. Ted noticed the tire tracks in the mud of the lane and the footprints leading from the pickup in the garage to the house. There was no doubt in his mind that Darrell Baird was the culprit. He knocked on the door. Darrell answered it in his robe and slippers.

"Darrell, I'm just gonna ask you straight: Did you dynamite the Nippon building last night?"

"What if I did?" Darrell said defiantly. "They had it comin.' You don't know the atrocities I seen in the South Pacific that them Japs committed. Settin' their building program back a few days is small compensation."

"Darrell, you need to get dressed and come with me," Ted said in an even voice.

"I figured as much," Darrell said, and disappeared into a back room. He returned in less than five minutes, hauling up the straps on his bib overalls. He still wore his house slippers. They left the house, and Ted opened the car door for Darrell. He climbed in without a word.

"You takin' me to jail, Ted?" he asked, as they headed up the interstate.

"Just for a few days," the marshal answered. "Just until we have a chance to get this mess cleared up. You'll be safer here."

They drove to the county seat, and Darrell was put into a cell.

"Now, you feed this guy anything he wants," Ted said to the jailer. "The town'll pay for it. I'll be back in a few days to claim him."

He turned to Darrell. "And don't give 'em any trouble. You're in enough already."

In the next three weeks the damage to the building was repaired. The men who worked on it, along with the townsfolk, were unaware of a greater reparation taking place in the county jail. When Mr. Tsukamoto heard of the vandalism and the man who committed it, he said to his secretary, "I'll be out for the afternoon." He got his driver to take him to the county jail, where he asked to see Darrell Baird.

Entering the cell, he extended his hand. "Mr. Baird, I'm Mr. Tsukamoto of Nippon America."

"I know who you are," Darrell said sullenly, still sitting on his bed.

"May I sit down?"

"Suit yourself," Darrel said. He sat up. "I reckon I know what you come for—to give me Hell for blowin' up your plant. Well, go ahead. Get it off yer chest."

Mr. Tsukamoto sat on the only seat in the cell, a wooden stool.

"Mr. Baird, I came to tell you a story, my own story. When I was a boy, our family lived in California. After Japan bombed Pearl Harbor, we were taken to a camp with other Japanese Americans and kept there for four years. We had done nothing against America, but the government feared us. So they locked us up to control us.

"The conditions were not good there. It was poor and dirty, and the food was not what we wanted. We were treated like the enemy. Sometimes if a person complained, he was beaten. It was a very hard life, and I vowed to leave America if I got the chance.

"After the war, we were released, but my parents were bitter against America. We went back to Japan. My father tried to help restore our country. But there was much sickness, and in two years he died. My mother and I went to live with her sister at Yokohama, away from the radiation. I grew up there and went to work at an electronics plant, making transistors. That's how I came to start Nippon America. I wanted to come back and try to establish a new relationship with the country I had hated as a child."

Darrell stared at the floor and shifted on his bed.

"Mr. Baird, I could not go on hating America the rest of my life. I knew it would make my heart sick. It would ruin my life. Japan is rebuilding, and now America is our friend. It took a lot of forgiveness on both sides, but I think our wounds are healing. I have come to ask your forgiveness for our part in the war. I hope we can be friends."

Darrell looked up to see Mr. Tsukamoto smiling.

"My forgiveness?"

"I can't live among people who hate me," Tsukamoto said. "I know that our nation did some terrible things in the war. So I have to ask forgiveness—for all of Japan."

"Well, maybe I've carried this thing around too long," Darrell said at last, looking at the floor again. Then he lifted his head. "I guess the atom bomb was pretty terrible, too. Killed a lot of people. I hope your country can forgive us for that. But it seemed like the only solution at the time."

They were both silent for a moment, then Mr. Tsukamoto said quietly, "Thank you. I needed to hear it. I can go now."

He stood, and Darrell stood with him.

"Thanks for comin' to see me. That took a lot of guts."

"It was the right thing to do," Mr. Tsukamoto replied. He offered his hand, and Darrell shook it.

"Please come to see me when you can," Tsukamoto said. "We'll have lunch together. Japanese or American, whichever you prefer."

For the first time in many years, Darrell Baird smiled—a happy smile, free of the pent-up anger he had carried for fifteen years.

"I'll do it," he said.

Through the winter months the work continued inside the Nippon building. Curiosity grew among the folks of Thornburg about the modern equipment and its capabilities. They were delighted to learn that the day after Easter was a Grand Opening; the community was invited to visit the new facility. Folks came throughout the day, taking the guided tour, marveling at the machinery, the offices, the immaculate assembly room that looked more like a hospital than a factory.

"They sure hate dirt here," one woman said.

"I always thought . . ." another began, then abruptly stopped.

"What?"

"Oh, nothing I guess," she answered. Then she pointed to a large photograph on an office wall. "That must be their home plant. Looks nice. Like it could be in America."

The five Japanese families who settled in Thornburg that year bought houses in town, and their children went to school with their neighbors. On the first day of classes, a Japanese first grader held the hand of an American classmate as they walked together down the street. Their mothers watched anxiously from their front yards.

"Already they are friends," observed the Japanese mother, and the Thornburg mother nodded in appreciation.

The town eventually learned that foreigners are not necessarily frightening or dangerous, that the past does not need to determine the present. Old prejudices dropped slowly away as the new Americans took their place alongside the Scots and Germans and English who had settled the land. In time the children did date one another, and one Japanese-American couple married and stayed in town to raise their family.

"Because," they said, "a small town is really the best place for children to grow up, whether in Japan or America. And this one is home."

The Trouble with Fences

In 1959, a developer from the county seat convinced the Thornburg Town Council that a subdivision of newer homes would go a long way toward keeping younger families in town. He offered to buy the woodland on the southeast corner of Main Street and County Road 100 S and develop it into half-acre lots. In order that they wouldn't look like the cookie-cutter homes in many other subdivisions, he showed them house plans for three different styles.

"I think you'll find, as I have in other housing developments, that folks like the ranch-style home best," he said. "These three basic plans offer six possible styles; each of them can be built as a mirror image of itself. There's room for twenty homes on that acreage. I don't think we'd have any trouble selling them. People are looking for quiet towns like this one, and I know you'd like to keep some younger families in the area."

The property had never been cleared. An assortment of trees grew there, most of which were not useful as lumber. The fifty-seven acres belonged to the adjoining farm; the owner was glad to get a good price for it. The council approved the plan. So that summer, bulldozers came and pushed down the trees and shrubs, and huge trucks hauled them away. The land was leveled, ditched for sewer pipe and water lines, and construction of the houses began.

The plan was to build two entrances: one from the state highway and one from the county road. The street through the subdivision formed an ell, with one cul-de-sac. The houses were well built. The first three were sold by September, even before they were finished. By Christmas, only two houses were still in a state of construction, and they sold in January. Four couples who lived in older homes in town moved into their new dwellings in early March while the yards were still only mud. But the new residents were as happy as though the lawns were green and planted with trees.

Rose and Ed McKinley had lived next door to David and Lydia Parker on Clarion Street. Now they bought adjacent houses in Woodland Acres, as the new subdivision was named. Brad and Patty Munson came from the other side of town, leaving Patty's ancestral home on Barton Road to move in beside them. Marlin and Julia Parsons bought one of the homes in the cul-de-sac. Don and Carla Belson and Ray and Myra Spencer bought adjoining lots at the east end, next to the Kagawas. Two couples from out of town moved into houses at the west end. By the next Christmas, lawns were well established, and the families tried to outdo each other in decorating their properties.

Rose McKinley stood in her front yard on Christmas Eve, ankle-deep in snow, and called to her husband to come out and see the lights. The subdivision glowed like a fairy forest. A feeling of peace prevailed. They could see their neighbors' trees through the picture windows.

Lights hung on bushes that were hardly more than nursery stock, yet everything had a Christmas air about it.

David and Lydia came out to stand with them until they got too cold to gaze any longer. "Come on over and have popcorn and apples with us!" Lydia said. "It's an old family tradition on Christmas Eve." And they did.

The next spring, the neighbors were busy tending their luxuriant lawns, planting more trees and shrubs, and talking with each other about the joys of suburban living.

"We don't have that draft in the bedroom we had in the old house," Patty Munson said. "And it's so great not having to run up and down stairs for everything!"

"Our old place in town was going to need a lot of repairs," Lydia said. "We figured it made more sense to start out new. The kids love the extra space and all the playmates around."

By summer, swings, slides, and jungle gyms went up in backyards throughout Woodland Acres. Children played at each other's homes. Families shared backyard picnics and barbeques. Sometimes a neighbor would mow the lawns on either side of his own, simply to show off his new riding mower. Friendships grew along with the grass and trees. The neighbors seemed inseparable. Woodland Acres was the growing edge of the community.

The trouble started one evening in spring when Patty Munson held up a page from the latest issue of *Better Homes & Gardens*.

"Look at this beautiful yard!" she exclaimed to her husband.

Brad looked away from the TV at the magazine and grunted, "Mm-hm."

"See how the morning glories and the trumpet creeper on the fence make a foil for the flowers in the beds along it?" Patty said. "I would love to have something like that." She looked at more of the pictures, then said, "Why couldn't we do that?"

"What?" he said, still staring at the TV.

"Like this picture of the fence and flowers. There's even a fishpond in the corner of the yard. That would be so neat!"

"That would be so expensive," he said. He looked at his wife. "You're talkin' five hundred dollars or more."

She was quiet as she read the article and gazed again at the pictures. She said nothing more about it until the weekend when they were at Sears and Roebuck in the county seat. She managed to steer her husband toward the yard equipment on the pretext of buying flowers, then pointed to the fencing.

"There's something almost identical to the fence in that magazine," she said. She went to it and touched it. "It would be beautiful along the side of our yard with flowering vines on it and beds of flowers in front. Oh! and look here!" She went to the corner of the enclosure where a pond had been set up. "We could do that. We could have a little goldfish pond. Marty and Bud would love it!"

"If they didn't fall in it," Brad said. He looked at the price posted above the pond: "$265 Installed."

"Couldn't we do without the pond?" he said. She could tell he was weakening.

"I wonder how big our yard is," she said, ignoring the question.

"I think it's about fifty by sixty," he said.

"Oh, I think it's bigger than that," she said. "More like sixty by seventy-five." She had already measured it.

"Maybe," he said. He thought a minute. "That'd be two hundred and ten feet of fence, plus whatever it takes to join it to the house. You're talking big bucks there."

"Let's find out," she said, and went to find a salesman.

Eventually, she talked him into it. They left with promise of delivery on Wednesday, and Brad drove home with the specter of debt haunting him.

On Wednesday morning a huge truck pulled into Woodland Acres and stopped at the Munson home. Two men got out and came to the door. In a few minutes they began to unload fencing onto the driveway. An astonishing sight met the neighbors as they came home from work.

"What on earth are you doing?" Rose McKinley gasped, "building a barn?"

"Just a fence," Patty said. "It's for flowers to grow on—you know, morning glories, trumpet creeper, things like that. We'll put in beds of flowers against it and a fish pond in the back corner."

Rose stared at the pile of lumber and tried to imagine the change it would make in the subdivision. Finally she said, "Well, I hope it's as pretty as you think it'll be."

Lydia and David came over when they arrived from work and had much the same response as Rose. "We won't be able to see you over the top!" David said. "Our kids will have to use a gate or something, I guess."

Patty had not thought of that. If she had flowers and a fishpond, she might not want children playing in the yard. Maybe they could build a chain-link enclosure for the swings and slide. Bud and Marty could play there. The cost of the adventure was beginning to add up in her head.

By Saturday of the following week the fence was done. In the meantime, Brad parked his car in the McKinleys' driveway. Now it seemed to Patty that she had walled herself off from the entire world. The boards extended eight feet above the ground, their tops cut into fleur-de-lis designs. When they were joined to the house, the backyard looked like a prison.

"It'll take some getting used to," she said, trying to assuage her fears. "But I think when we get some vines crawling on it and some flowers in front of it, it'll look just like the picture."

"Hope so," Brad said.

Patty busied herself all the next week planting clematis, trumpet creeper, morning glory, and a pink-flowered vine she could never pronounce correctly. But the man at the nursery assured her they would all grow on the fence and look gorgeous together. She bought a pot of Shasta daisies to put near the house, up against the fence. Then she set out an assortment of plants in front of it.

Brad came out to inspect the plantings, nodded approval, and turned to look at the back of the yard.

"We're gonna need a shed for equipment," he said. "Know what I mean? Those little barns that you put lawn mowers in and rakes and stuff like that?"

"Well, maybe we can get one before the end of the season," Patty said. "I've been looking at the checkbook; it doesn't look too promising right now."

A knock sounded at the new gate beside the house. Rose opened it and came into the yard.

"Curiosity got the best of me," she said. "I had to see it from the inside."

"Welcome to the Munson Botanical Gardens," Brad said. "Of course, you have to imagine a lot."

"By this time next year, you'll be green with envy," Patty exulted. "We want to put a goldfish pond in that corner. Won't that be fun!"

"But you can't let your kids play out here, can you?" Rose said. "I'd be afraid they'd fall in the pond, or destroy the flowers."

"We're—well, *I'm* thinking that we can build a chain-link enclosure around the swings and slide and sandbox, so the kids won't be in any danger. Brad says it'll make them look like animals in a cage, but I don't think they'll mind."

Rose said nothing and walked to the fence, closely observing the new plantings. "These trumpet vines?" she asked.

"Yes," Patty said. "I love their orange flowers. And there'll be several colors of morning glories among them, with purple clematis on the corners."

"Should be nice," Rose said, "but I'm afraid we won't see you guys as often, with the fence up."

"Oh, sure you will!" Patty said. "We'll just use our front doors instead of our back doors."

"Well, you sure have started a big project," Rose said. "See you later." She left by the gate and closed it carefully behind her.

"I don't know what they're planning to do over there," she said to her husband, "but I bet it's more than flowers and fishponds. Patty's always talking about the lack of privacy in the neighborhood, kids running through the backyards, people walking by and looking into windows. We've never bothered them, as far as I know. I mean, she never said anything about it before."

"Maybe it isn't us," Ed replied. "Maybe they just want privacy. Maybe she wants to sunbathe in the nude or something."

"Now, wouldn't you like that!" his wife said. "I can see you now, boring a hole in the fence."

"Well, at any rate it's none of our business," he said.

But Rose and Ed weren't the only ones talking about the fence. They talked with the Parkers on the other side and agreed the thing was an eyesore in the neighborhood.

"You can't see through the yards anymore," Rose complained. "I can't tell if my kids are playing on the Cox's jungle gym unless I walk around the Munsons' fence. If we had a neighborhood cookout, we'd have to carry everything around that monstrosity."

The Parkers said it seemed almost as if the Munsons had seceded from the community. Throughout Woodland Acres, judgments were leveled against the fence until the Munsons were considered "out of the circle." Since they lived on the west end of the subdivision, they were not invited to many gatherings on the east end—"because I know it's so far to walk," one woman said to Patty. "Anyway, I know you folks down there are close, aren't you?"

Later that week, Rose had another thought. Maybe the fence was Brad's idea after all. Maybe *he's* the one peeping through a hole in the fence, watching *me* sunbathing—or Beverly Cox! It'd be just like him. I've never been comfortable with the way he looks at me. But she said nothing to Ed.

Two houses east of the Munsons lived Oren and Paula Berry. He was an attorney in the county seat. They were newcomers to Thornburg in the two years since Woodland Acres was built. They made friends slowly, but folks liked them and invited them to gatherings in the neighborhood. They had said nothing to anyone regarding the Munsons' fence.

In early June a backhoe drove onto their property and started to dig in their backyard. The few wives who worked at home stood in their own yards and watched the excavation, speculating about just what might be going on. The Berrys were not at home (Paula worked as a secretary in an office near her husband's law practice), so the neighbors could not ask them until they came home that evening. Bill and Beverly Cox strolled over casually after supper and knocked on their door.

"Hi, neighbor!" Bill said. "You guys through with supper?"

"Sure, come on in," Oren said. "How's it going?"

"Funny, that's what we were going to ask you," Bill said. "Couldn't help noticing the hole in your yard. You building another garage or what?"

"No, Paula and I have wanted a swimming pool for some time now, so we just decided to put one in."

"Wow!" Bill responded. "That's gonna be some pool! Must take up most of your backyard."

"Will it be deep?" Beverly asked.

"Three and a half feet at this end, ten at the other. We want enough water to dive into."

"You'll have to put a fence around it, won't you?" Beverly pursued. "To keep the kids out of it, I mean."

"Oh, yes," Oren said. "It'll have a chain-link fence around it and a gate and all. It'll be safe enough. You guys'll have to come over for a swim!"

"Sounds good," Bill said. "When do you think it'll be done?"

"They promise the fourth of July," Oren said, "but I'll be surprised if it's in by then. We still have to build a pool house and get the pump and filter installed. I'm guessing it won't be done before the middle of the month."

On the fourteenth of July the last of the workers left the Berrys' property, and several folks came over to see the finished product. The pump had been running steadily for three days to fill the pool. Oren had acquainted himself with the pump and filter, the chlorine tablets that floated on the surface of the water, and the usual maintenance requirements throughout the year. A chain-link fence surrounded the entire construction, including the pump house.

"Have you tried it out yet?" Bill asked as he walked around the perimeter of the pool. It was kidney-shaped; Paula had set out hostas in strategic spots along its edge.

"No, but we're going to try it out this evening," Oren said. "Paula wants it to be romantic the first time we go in, so we're going to have candlelight around the edge."

"Skinny dipping?" Bill asked with a grin.

"Too many interested neighbors," Oren said. "We plan to put up a privacy fence before summer's over."

Now the gossip caught fire and ran through the subdivision in less than a day. The Berrys were going to be skinny-dipping in their pool! Who knows what else! And children on both sides of them! Had they no shame?

And so, to protect their children from flagrant indecency, other families began to erect privacy fences in their own yards, forbidding their children from swimming in the Berrys' pool or even going into their yard.

"You read so much about kids drowning in backyard pools," Beverly Cox said to Robin Elliott one afternoon. "I just won't let Darrin and Steven go over there. The Berrys are never home in the daytime, anyway."

As summer moved into August, fewer and fewer cookouts were held, fewer gatherings across backyards (they were blocked by fences now), and fewer conversations among the neighbors. They had their own spaces, protected by wood and chain-link fences. They spent their time around their own pools or picnic tables. One or two families still associated together, yet it was not the same. Woodland Acres was no longer a community, it was a collection of separate dwellings, fenced off from one another for the sake of privacy at the cost of friendship and trust.

A family in the east end moved to Cincinnati at the behest of the husband's company, and it was two weeks before most of the families in the west end knew it. There had been no goodbyes, although the year before, the couple had been a regular part of the evening cookouts along the backyards. The neighborhood they had known was gone.

One has to wonder at the timing of events that change lives forever. They seem to come at moments of utter desperation, when life has stagnated and people are ripe for renewal and new perspective. At eleven minutes after ten o'clock on the night of August 21, a log truck loaded with white oak came east on County Road 100 S. The driver had spent the day a mile west of town with the men who cut the huge trunks and loaded them onto his flatbed trailer, securing them with chains. Now he was hoping to get a lot of road behind him before the sawmill opened at seven o'clock in the morning a hundred miles south. He was tired and sleepy and driving too fast for the gravel road.

By the time he got to the intersection with the state road, he had dozed off. The truck veered to the right as his hands relaxed on the wheel. The huge rig crossed the corner at Woodland Acres just south of the intersection. Thirty-six tons of lumber and steel hurtled across the ditch and into the backyards of the subdivision at forty miles an hour, tearing through fences as though they were made of paper, gouging deep ruts in the well-kept lawns, finally coming to a stop with the tractor hanging over the edge of the Berrys' swimming pool.

The chains that had held the logs broke when the truck jumped the ditch. Huge trunks thundered across the yards, tearing down fences, tool sheds, pump houses, and playground equipment. Patty Munson's flowers were utterly destroyed. Only the fishpond escaped damage.

The horrendous noise of shattering wood and falling logs woke the entire subdivision. People streamed out of their houses in nightclothes, pulling on robes, their eyes bulging with terror. Bill Cox got to the driver of the truck before anyone else and helped him out. He had to climb over the cab of the truck to avoid falling into the pool. The driver was unhurt, but badly shaken.

"What in God's name happened!" demanded Paula Berry.

"I think I must have dozed off," the driver said. "Was anyone hurt?"

"I don't know," Bill said, surveying the devastation. He and Oren ran along the backs of the houses, dodging splintered wood and twisted chain-link fencing, broken glass, and strewn logs. Yard lights had come on by now as people stood on their back steps and stared at the wreckage. Bill, who seemed to have more presence of mind than most, asked Brad Munson to call the marshal. Then he and Oren went back to see if the driver was OK.

The man was sitting on the Berrys' back step when Ted Bates arrived. The marshal looked everything over, making notes; he talked with the various neighbors who had come to stand around the truck and stare at the eerie scene.

"As far as you know, was anyone injured?" he asked Oren.

"Not that we can see."

"You OK?" Ted said to the driver. The man nodded his head. He was still in shock. Even though it was a warm night, Paula had draped a blanket across his shoulders. He occasionally shivered.

"Well, it's going to take bigger equipment than Thornburg has to get that truck and logs out of here," Ted said. "I'll call over to the county seat; they'll have it."

He took as much information as anyone could give him, then left in his car. Oren and Paula stood looking at their swimming pool with the truck cab suspended over it, the trailer stretched out behind it into the Cox's yard. The pump house was completely destroyed, the privacy fence in ruins. It looked like a scene from a science fiction film.

Bill Cox said to the driver, "Why don't you just stay with us tonight? They'll get the crane from the county seat tomorrow and put your rig back together."

The driver agreed, and the next afternoon when the crane and wreckers arrived, he helped direct the operation. The truck cab had not sunk into the pool but was still attached to the trailer, the word *Freightliner* half-submerged. Power winches towed the rig backward through the yards to the highway. The crane lifted the logs and loaded them onto a different truck sent by the logging company. A different driver took the wheel, and by evening he had left for the sawmill.

Huge tow trucks hauled off the damaged tractor and trailer.

The next morning the insurance adjuster for the entire subdivision arrived and assessed the damage.

"It'll take a lot of work to restore your properties," he told Brad Munson. "You and your neighbors need to make a list of all the stuff you lost—get your receipts if you still have them—and give me a call."

That evening the residents of Woodland Acres, even the ones whose properties were not involved in the accident, met in David and Lydia's home to talk. Brad told them what the insurance adjuster had said. They sat in silence a moment, then Oren said,

"You know, as I stood looking at the wreckage in my backyard, I thought how little damage it would have done if none of us had built fences and swimming pools. All it would have done was make ruts in the grass; that's easily fixed. Our homeowners policy is going to take a pretty heavy hit. I expect the premiums will go up."

"You gonna rebuild your fence and pool?" Bill asked.

"Paula and I talked about that," Oren said. "We don't think so. It wasn't nearly as romantic as we thought it would be. Fact is, we only skinny-dipped in it once. We felt too self-conscious, like maybe someone was looking over the fence at us. Besides, it was darned expensive to operate!"

Paula broke in, "The worst part, I think, is the distance these fences have put between us. I mean, a couple of years ago we were the best of friends, but the fences seem to have kept us apart. Privacy came at too high a price, I think."

"We've wondered the same thing," Patty said. "I wanted my yard to look like the one in *Better Homes & Gardens*, but I didn't realize it would separate me from all my friends. Gosh! We used to have such good times together at those cookouts! I miss 'em. We're going to put our yard back like it used to be."

They all agreed that no matter how much money they got for the damage to their property, they would not rebuild the fences.

"They just get in the way of everything," David Parker said. "I'd rather be able to see my neighbors, be able to holler across the backyards and feel like I'm part of a community. I guess I don't believe that old saying, 'Good fences make good neighbors.' "

"I don't think Robert Frost believed it, either," said Rose.

Starting Over

When Dixie Mae Crandall inherited her Aunt Clara's estate, she imagined several thousand dollars descending upon her like a beneficent rain. When she heard the will read and realized that her inheritance consisted of an eighty-year-old house in Thornburg, Indiana, and $500 in cash, she was speechless. Leaving the lawyer's office, she felt numb, desperate. She determined to go to Thornburg, visit the property, and arrange for its sale. At least she could realize some monetary benefit, maybe enough to get to Bermuda. Detroit was a dead end for her; somehow she had to escape it. Forty years there had left her nothing but misery.

She arrived in Thornburg on the Tuesday afternoon bus, looking around at the strangest place she had ever seen. Not a building stood more than two stories high. No buses plowed the streets, no taxies honked and bullied their way through hoards of automobiles, no masses of pedestrians raced the lights and traffic across intersections. She walked to the corner carrying her suitcase, hoping to find women like herself from whom she might elicit information. There were none.

There were also no bars in which she might inquire. She saw the Town Hall with the Marshal's Office next door, and shunned it. She had had enough of the law.

At last she went into the drugstore and asked Doyle Case the way to 313 South Wood Street. He told her how to find it, and she left without even saying Thank You. It had not been in her vocabulary for many years.

She found Wood Street and 313, and came to a dead stop. The house was old and brown, two facts which repulsed her. She went to the front porch, groping in her purse for the key the lawyer had given her. A strange aroma met her as she opened the door and stepped into the living room: a closed-up, musty odor of old furniture, old curtains, old carpet. She had not been in the house since she was a child of six. She remembered nothing about it. Too much had intervened in the years between.

The smell of an old woman's things curled her nostrils. She set the suitcase down and walked into the dining room. A built-in cupboard in the wall held antique glassware and china; the table and chairs were vintage 1920s.

"Early American Attic," she said to herself.

The kitchen had not been updated since the invention of the refrigerator, which stood silent against the far wall, its door propped open for ventilation. Someone obviously had cleaned out the foodstuffs from it. The cupboards were empty. She wondered whom her Aunt Clara had known who would take on a task like that.

Upstairs the bedrooms were neat and clean, the beds made. Linens in the hall closet were folded and neatly stacked. "Some fanatic old broad!" she said aloud, and went back downstairs and sat on the sofa.

"Well," she said to no one, "I guess this is home—at least for tonight."

Tomorrow she would look up a realtor and put the house on the market. She wondered what it would bring, if it would be enough to get to Bermuda and live for a while. She had no plan beyond that dream. She was tired in body and soul. Life had not gone the way she envisioned in high school. Her father's absence from the family, her mother's self-pity, and her own craving for love had driven her into a world of risk and submission. She had sold her self-respect for a chance at a miracle, but the miracle had not happened.

She decided at last to see this infinitesimal town into which she had been thrust. Leaving her suitcase sitting in the living room, she locked the front door behind her. She walked up Wood Street to Jefferson, then west to Main, strolling up the east side to look in the windows. She had imagined fashion shops, shoe stores, jewelry stores, but Myrtie's Dress Shop across the street was the nearest thing to them. She crossed over and looked in. Nothing there looked like the clothes she had on: a low-cut blouse, a full skirt of rayon in gaudy colors, and bright red strap sandals with four-inch heels.

Dixie realized she was out of place in this plain and simple town, yet it was the only place she had now. She had skipped out on her apartment in Detroit owing three months' rent. She couldn't go back there. She didn't want to. She didn't know what she wanted, except to start life over someplace else. Bermuda, preferably. Maybe she could get a job there. She had no skills except the one profession that had bought her groceries for twenty years. It had not brought her friendship or joy. It had used her up. She felt crumpled, wadded, discarded, like an empty cigarette package. The joy of living had abandoned her many years ago. She had settled for survival.

Strolling west on Jefferson, she came to Bennett's Park and sat on one of the benches there. It was a pleasant afternoon in May, the kind of day that brings pleasure to most people. But to Dixie it seemed empty and hopeless. She had never felt so alone. If she had not forsworn tears two decades ago, she would have cried. Instead, she sat and stared at the fields beyond the town limits. They seemed like the end of the world to her. Her aunt's legacy was the one thing that had kept her from suicide, and that might not last long. Singing birds in nearby trees brought her no delight; the pleasant air was lost to her.

At last she resolved to look up a realtor yet that afternoon and see if she could get the sale of the house moving. The sooner the better. She walked back to Main Street and looked up and down both sides. Returning to the drug store, she asked Doyle where she might find a realtor.

"You need to talk to Paul Besser," he told her. "He handles the real estate in town." He wrote the address on a piece of notepaper and handed it to her. "Just down the street and around the corner on Walnut."

She took the paper and left the store, turning at Walnut until she found the address. She knocked and waited. An elderly gentleman came to the door.

"Yes?"

"The guy at the drugstore told me you handle the real estate in town."

"Well, he's right. I'm Paul Besser. Would you like to come in?"

She entered and stood by the door.

"My aunt left me her house in her will, and I want to sell it," she said. "It's 313 South Wood Street."

"Oh, yes, I know that house well. Your aunt Clara Morgan was a lovely woman. She was our librarian for more than thirty years, you know. I'm sorry for your loss."

"How much ya think it's worth?" Dixie asked, ignoring his sympathy.

"Well, we'll have to see. Wouldn't you like to sit down?"

"No, I just want to get it on the market. Do you need to look it over?"

"No, I think we'll just put a notice in the paper and a sign in the yard. That should do it," he said, smiling. "Will you be staying there?"

"Sure. I got no place else. Come see me when you know something."

"I certainly will," he said, and she left.

Paul Besser made the usual necessary inquiries into title and abstract at the courthouse in the county seat and put a For Sale notice in the newspaper. The next afternoon he hammered a red and white sign in the front yard.

This House For Sale

Paul Besser, Realtor.

Dixie found Barclay's Restaurant and ate supper alone in a corner. Joyce, a pretty teenage girl, waited on her, making the usual small talk.

Dixie answered in one word responses, and the girl eventually left her alone. Before she was finished eating, George Barclay, the owner of the establishment, came over to see if she needed anything else. She was fine, she said.

"You new in town or just passin' through?" he inquired.

"I'll be here a while," Dixie said. "My Aunt Clara Morgan left me her house. I've got it up for sale. When it sells, I'll be gone."

She said it in a fatalistic tone of voice, as though it were foreordained.

"Well, you're sure welcome to stay in Thornburg," Barclay told her. "Let us know if you need anything."

She paid her bill and left and, having no place else to go, went back to the house. It seemed to her like a tomb, the end of her life, unless its sale could launch her into another climate, another world where she might find whatever it was that made people happy. Nothing in her forty years had been able to do that.

As she got ready to climb into one of the beds upstairs, she looked at herself in the mirror over the dresser. Her eyes were tired and drawn, her figure sagged. She had always prided herself on her looks; now she saw only a worn-out woman, old beyond her years. She undressed on the other side of the room to avoid her naked body in the mirror. Then she turned out the light and got into bed. The room seemed stuffy, so she got up and opened a window. The sound of a night bird came to her through the darkness, accentuating her loneliness. She got back into bed, and for the first time in twenty years she turned her face into the pillow and sobbed.

On Friday morning, Ted Bates got a call from the Metropolitan Police in Detroit, inquiring if a Miss Dixie Mae Crandall had arrived in town. Ted said that she had. The realtor had told him that she had moved into her aunt's house left to her in the will. Was there a problem?

"Well, there's a claim against the estate for $225 back rent on an apartment here," the sergeant said. "Naturally, we don't want to come down there to collect it; I wonder if you could handle it."

"Sure," Ted said. "Send me the paper work. I'll go talk to her."

The necessary papers were in the Monday morning mail. Ted read them over carefully. It seemed that Dixie had a police record for prostitution, had done some jail time, and had left owing three months' rent for her apartment. He went to her house and knocked on the door. She opened it warily, noticing Ted's uniform.

"What's the problem, officer?"

"Are you Dixie Mae Crandall?"

"Yeah, what's the problem?"

"Miss Crandall, I had a call from the Detroit police that there's a claim against your aunt's estate—yours now, I guess—for $225 back rent on an apartment. You know anything about that?"

"I shoulda known it would catch up with me," she sighed. "So what do I do, give it to you? It's about all I have. She only left me $500 besides the house."

"Well, Miss Crandall, you have a couple of options: you can send the money to your creditor in Detroit, or you can call up there and make some kind of arrangement to pay it off in installments. They might do that. But if you don't do something to pay it off, I'm afraid the law will come down here to collect it."

Dixie stood grimly in the doorway, her teeth clenched. She hadn't thought the landlord would pursue her this far. She hadn't realized how information regarding her past would be so available. Even in Thornburg, Indiana!

"I'll pay it," she said. "I don't know what I'll eat on, but I'll give you the money. I don't have a bank account, so I can't send a check."

"I can't collect it for them," Ted said. "But you can buy a money order at the post office and send it. You'd better do that yet today. I'll call the department and tell them it's on the way."

"Look," she said, "I'm tryin' to start over, and I haven't got much to go on. Just this house. As soon as I can sell it, I'll be out of here. I'm just tryin' to stay out of trouble."

"I understand," Ted said. "I'm sorry it's making a hardship for you, but I can't get around the law. I hope you understand."

"I'll get the money in the mail," she said, and closed the door.

After the marshal had gone, Dixie found the post office on Jefferson Street, shelled out $225 plus the fee, and sent a money order to her former landlord. By now she had less than $200 in her purse.

Someone passing through the marshal's office in the afternoon noticed the papers on his desk and glanced at them. Dixie's photo was stapled to the top left corner; the person recognized her from seeing her on the street. Her bleached blonde hair and low-cut neckline stood out in this conservative little town. Noted, too, were the police record, the jail time, and the word "prostitution." By suppertime a dozen other people knew it, as is the way in small towns.

At breakfast on Saturday morning, as Dixie sat in Barclay's Restaurant, other customers noticeably avoided her. She couldn't help seeing people staring at her in the grocery, dropping their heads as they passed her on the street. Just as I expected, she thought. I can't get out of this town soon enough.

In the afternoon she went back to the park. As she sat on the bench under the tree, a man came and sat on the other end. He had followed her from town. She was used to men following her.

"You need something?" she asked him.

"Well," he began, "I couldn't help noticing that you seem to be alone in town. I thought you might have questions or need help of some kind." He hesitated a moment while Dixie assessed him, then he said, "Everything OK with you?"

"So far," she answered. "What's your name?"

"Oh, I'm just one of the guys in town."

"And what kind of help are you offering?"

"Well, I hear you're a–professional. I, uh, just wondered if you'd like to make a little money."

Dixie stood and turned toward the man, her face set and defiant.

"Listen, Buster, I left that life in Detroit. So you can forget about it, OK?"

"OK," he said, and shrugged his shoulders, looking away.

She walked back into town. Would it be this way everywhere? Would she never be free of her past? How could she change what she had been if all people ever saw was a prostitute? Couldn't anyone see her as a person, someone with feelings and hopes and dreams like everyone else? She went back home in case someone came to inquire about the house.

The next morning shimmered with the light of late May. Dixie decided to visit her aunt's grave, more out of curiosity than sentiment. She had seen the tops of tombstones west of the park, across the railroad and Bode's Creek. She walked to the cemetery and strolled among the stones barefooted until she came to the mound of a recent burial. The new stone at the head of the grave read simply, "Clara Morgan 1880-1961." Dixie stood a moment looking at the stone. Other graves nearby were marked with stones bearing the name Morgan, relatives Dixie had never heard of.

Her mother had told her almost nothing about the family. She knew only that her parents had divorced when Dixie was five. Clara was her mother's only sister, older by fifteen years and never married.

Dixie looked at other stones, names unfamiliar to her, and walked back into town.

No one inquired about the house. Dixie began to feel desperate. The end of June was approaching; she knew she had to find a job. The only people she had talked to since her arrival were the pharmacist, the realtor, the restaurant owner, and the marshal. She needed a friend, but it didn't seem likely that she would find one among these strangers.

And then, in the way such things happen, in the normal pattern of daily living, one came to her.

More out of boredom than interest, Dixie entered the Thornburg Library at Wood and Prospect Streets on a Thursday afternoon to see where her aunt had worked. She browsed the magazine rack. She strolled around and looked at the stacks neatly categorized according to the Dewey Decimal System. She had spent so little time in libraries that she had no idea how to find a book, or even if she would be allowed to check one out. She was not a reader in the popular sense.

The librarian, Marcella Pratt, came to her and asked, "Are you looking for something in particular?" She smiled pleasantly at Dixie Mae.

"No, I—uh—just wanted to get acquainted with the town," Dixie answered. "My aunt used to be the librarian here."

"You're Clara Morgan's niece!" Marcella exclaimed. "I'm so glad to meet you! I heard you were in town."

"Yeah, I came here to sell the house, but it's taking longer than I thought."

"Well, we hope you'll decide to stay in town after all," Marcella said. "This is a wonderful place to live! You'd have a lot of friends here."

Dixie smiled faintly and answered, "I doubt it. I've never had a lot of friends—anywhere. No, what I need is a job of some kind to keep me going until the house sells. You know of anything?"

"Well, let me think," Marcella said. "I'm sure someone in town needs help. I could use some right here in the library, as a matter of fact."

"I don't know anything about libraries," Dixie said. She looked around. "I don't read much."

"Well, Dear, reading isn't a requirement for putting books on shelves. What I need, if the Library Board will okay it, is someone to help me get the books ready for shelving, cull out the ones that no one reads, things like that. It's mostly a matter of an extra pair of hands. If you're interested, I'd be happy to have you."

Dixie looked at her open and trusting face, wondering how long it would be before Marcella found out about her past and fired her.

"I'll think about it," she told Marcella. She turned at the door and said, "Thanks for asking."

The Library Board had confidence in Marcella, but they warned her that a woman "with her past" might not be the best choice for a library assistant.

"But she needs an income," Marcella protested, "and I don't know anyone else who will hire her."

"Well, there's a reason for that," the board chairman said. "She's spent time in jail up in Detroit for prostitution. Did you know that?"

"I'm aware of her history," Marcella countered. "The whole town is. I believe she needs a friend. She seems to be at her wits' end. I'd like to see if we can help her."

"The best way to help her is to find someone to buy that house," a woman volunteered.

"I'm thinking that she isn't likely to find the kind of people she needs if it isn't in a town like Thornburg," Marcella said. "She's doing her best to change her life. We need to help her."

The board finally agreed that if Marcella was willing to be responsible for her, they would agree to a one month trial period. There was no doubt that Marcella needed help in the library. Since Clara Morgan had died, Marcella had had a hard job of it, reorganizing the library and getting rid of things Clara had allowed to accumulate over the years. She went to Dixie's home that evening and told her the news.

"You can start tomorrow," she said. "The board agreed to a one month trial period. I know we're going to get on just fine! You'll learn quickly, I can tell."

That evening Marcella's phone rang. It was Emojean Billings.

"Marcella, I hope what I heard is not true: that you're thinking of hiring that woman from Detroit. Do you know what she is? She's a *prostitute*. We don't need that kind living in Thornburg."

"Emojean," Marcella said quietly, "the world is hard enough without our making it harder for folks like Dixie. She's making a real effort to change her life, and there's no better place to do it than Thornburg. I think we have a lot to offer her, don't you? I can tell she'll do well at the library. She has a good mind and, I believe, a good heart."

"I don't know what you expect of her," Emojean said. "All she knows is the street. You can't make a silk purse out of—"

"We have to do our best to accept her and support her," Marcella broke in. "If no one cares about her, tries to help her, what chance does she have?"

"Well, I can tell you right now she's not spending any time around *my* husband!"

"I don't think she's interested in anyone's husband," Marcella said. "She's interested in a job, and I intend to give her one. I hope you'll get to know her and try to be her friend. She needs friends."

Mrs. Billings sighed and said, "Well, for your sake I'll try to be nice to her. But I warn you, a leopard doesn't change its spots, my father always said."

"Well, if she were a leopard, I guess we'd have cause to worry," Marcella laughed. "Let's give her a chance, be friendly, help her out. It's the least we can do—for Clara's sake if nothing else. She evidently had confidence in her, or she wouldn't have left her the house."

"I suppose so. Well, we'll see."

Mrs. Billings hung up.

Working in books and learning the Dewey Decimal System was the farthest thing imaginable from Dixie's former occupation. But at least it would give her a small paycheck each week. Right now that was all that mattered. She found that the work was not as burdensome as she had supposed. Working with Marcella was much pleasanter than sitting alone in her house or walking the streets. She and Marcella talked of many things. Marcella gently introduced subjects she was interested in and asked Dixie of her interests. She didn't pry into Dixie's past but left the door open for Dixie to share whatever she cared to.

"How much family do you have?" Marcella asked her one morning.

"Just my mother. She lives in Michigan, but we don't communicate anymore."

"I'm sorry," Marcella said with a genuine sympathy.

"It's OK," Dixie said. "She never approved of me anyway."

Marcella seemed thoughtful for a while.

At length she said, "I have a daughter that I'm afraid I haven't always understood. I try to stay in touch—she lives in North Carolina—but her world seems quite different from mine. She's an artist and lives with a man she's not married to. I love her, of course, but she doesn't want to be close. We exchange Christmas cards. Sometimes I call to see how she is."

She sighed and seemed to be lost in her thoughts.

Dixie copied Dewey Decimal numbers onto title pages, as Marcella had taught her. Presently she said, "I wish it could be easier."

"What, Dear?"

"Talking to people, being close. I don't think I've ever really been close to anyone. Life seems like a—I don't know what—like a cheat, I guess. The people who cross your path just use you, and that's the end of it. I never had a friend I could count on. One of the girls. . . ." She stopped speaking and picked up another book.

Marcella waited a space, then said, "I believe we have to take the people God sends us."

Dixie stopped her work and looked up. "You what?"

"I think He does it for a reason," Marcella went on, "even if we don't know what it is. If we open ourselves to friendship, I think there must be no end to the possibilities."

"No end to the pain," Dixie answered. She laid down the book and leaned against the wall with a hand on her hip. Looking directly at Marcella she said, "I was a prostitute in Detroit for twenty years. I've been used and abused by more men and women than you've ever seen. If I seem not to believe in this "God" who sends us people to be our friends, it's because I was never sent one I could trust."

Marcella took Dixie's hands in her own and said gently, "Dixie, I'm so sorry for the way you've been treated. But in spite of the pain it's caused you, it's past now. It's gone. Sure, it left some scars, but you're still young. You can heal. It takes time and trust, and God doesn't leave us alone. He always sends someone to help."

"Well, He sure takes His old sweet time about it," Dixie said. She turned her face away as a tear made its way down her cheek.

"Well," Marcella sighed, "I guess it's been a long time coming, but here we are."

"Meaning what?" Dixie wiped her face with the back of her hand.

"I believe God sent you to me, and maybe me to you. We need each other, I think. We both have a lot to give. Maybe working with you will help me understand my daughter. Maybe I can help you in some way."

"I think it's too late for me," Dixie said. She sat down on a chair. "This town will never accept me. I'm the news right now. As soon as I can sell the house, I'll have to move on."

Marcella drew her chair close to Dixie's and looked kindly into her eyes.

"Dear, half the people in this town have something in their past they're not proud of. We live with each other because we need the strength of community. None of us can make it alone. There isn't a perfect person here. Oh, one or two think they are, but we've all made our mistakes. We just learn from them. They're part of being human."

She offered Dixie a Kleenex and continued, "Do you think God loves only perfect people? My stars! There wouldn't be a one of us left to love if that were so!"

Dixie sat and sobbed until she was exhausted. Marcella leaned over and put her arms around her. She yielded to the comfort of it and laid her head against Marcella's. They sat together for several minutes in silence.

At length Dixie said, "I always hoped love would come from some guy that wanted me for myself, not just my body. But I could never find him. Just now, what you said about God sending us people to love—Well, I just hope it's true. I've always wanted my mother's love, but I never felt it. I don't think she wanted a child. I was a mistake. She put up with me until I was sixteen. I think she was glad when I ran away from home. She didn't try to find me. By the time she knew where I was. . . ." She shook her head and wiped her eyes.

"No one is a mistake, Dixie," Marcella said gently. "Some of us came at inopportune times, or were born to people who didn't know what they were doing. But God doesn't make mistakes. You're His child as much as anyone on this earth. His love includes you as well as me and everyone you meet."

"How can you know that? I mean, how can you be sure God loves you—if there is a God?"

"If love were not real, then I think we wouldn't feel the need for it," Marcella answered. "We wouldn't respond to it when it comes to us. We wouldn't have the urge to reach out toward others and give what we can. It's what Jesus was all about, to wake us up to that fact."

Dixie was quiet a while. At last she said, "I never had much to do with that church stuff. It always seemed to leave me out. I knew I wasn't good enough to be there."

"Love isn't about institutions, Dixie, it's about a gift God has given every one of us. If being good was the requirement, I'm afraid most of us would be left out."

They sat quietly a moment, then Dixie said weakly, "I don't think I've ever been loved. Not really. Not by anyone."

Without hesitation, Marcella said, "*I* love you, Dixie. Partly because you need someone to love you, and partly because I need someone to love. My son and daughter-in-law live here in town, but they have their jobs and three children to care for. She's a teacher and he works in Cranfield as an insurance adjuster for the Farm Bureau, so we don't have much time together. Your coming to the library has been a Godsend for me."

Dixie's face slowly opened into a smile. She looked at Marcella as one looks at a sunrise.

"No one, in all my life, ever told me they loved me," she said through her tears. Her face began to relax. The wrinkles that had etched nearly permanent furrows in her brow softened in trust toward this genuine person who had been drawn into her life. She put both arms around Marcella and hugged her, saying over and over, "Thank you! Thank you!"

When Marcella reported to the library board that Dixie was working out "splendidly," they agreed she could stay as a permanent employee.

"But she's under your guidance," a board member warned her. "If she gets in trouble, she'll have to go."

"That girl needs all the love and acceptance this town can muster," Marcella said with conviction. "I expect every one of you to support her, get to know her. She needs friends. None of us can make it in this world without friends."

In the weeks that followed, Dixie took her house off the market, put in a telephone, and bought new curtains for the windows. She bought two pairs of blue jeans and some summer blouses, and "sensible shoes" as Marcella called them. Marcella introduced her to the patrons of the library as they came in. Over the months of summer, many in Thornburg came to know Dixie as "Marcella's girl." She proved to be a lot more intelligent than she knew. Soon she was as familiar with the Dewey Decimal System as Marcella was, and she learned to speak with the library patrons knowledgeably and helpfully.

"Well, maybe I was wrong about her," Emojean Billings said to Clarice Brooks at lunch one day. Marcella seems to dote on her. She must have something on the ball."

"She's certainly made that house of Clara's shine," Clarice said. "Have you been inside it?"

"No, but I'd love to see it. Clara left it in a shambles, you remember. If the neighbors hadn't gone in and cleaned it up, it'd be unlivable. You think she'd let us in?"

"I don't know why not. Why don't we take her something? Kind of a house-warming."

So the next afternoon Emojean and Clarice went to the library and asked Dixie if they might visit in her home that evening.

"We just want to stop by for a few minutes and get acquainted," they said.

"Well, sure, that would be OK," Dixie said.

"Can you believe that!" she exclaimed to Marcella. "I'm going to have company!"

Around seven o'clock that evening, the two women rang Dixie's doorbell. When she opened the door, there they stood holding platters covered with dishtowels.

"We couldn't come empty-handed," Clarice said. She set her platter on Dixie's sideboard in the dining room. Emojean put hers beside it.

"They're just some cookies and things we made," Clarice said. "Oh, and Mrs. Devington sent along a jar of her homemade preserves. She goes into the fields every June and picks raspberries and makes jam. It's always delicious!"

"Well, thank you!" Dixie said it sincerely, and uncovered the platters. There were four or five kinds of cookies, brownies, and Elnora Devington's jar of jam. Beside them was a card with flowers on the front. She picked it up and opened it. It said,

"Sorry for the belated welcome to Thornburg! We're glad you decided to stay."

It was signed by all the women of the Thornburg Women's Quilting and Knitting Circle.

"Maybe you'd like to join us," Emojean said. "We meet every Saturday afternoon to quilt, but some of us just knit at home or do needlework. And then there's a craft fair every year. It's coming up soon."

"I'm not much of a joiner," Dixie said, "but I need to make friends. Maybe I'll try it."

"Well, you can let us know."

They stayed long enough to see the improvements Dixie had made in the house and to congratulate her on her good taste, not knowing how much input Marcella Pratt had had in the project. When they left, Dixie smiled for a full five minutes. For the first time in her life she felt at home. Maybe, after all, she *could* belong someplace.

On Saturday afternoon she met with the Quilting and Knitting Circle in the basement of the Christian Church, just to get acquainted. She knew nothing about any of it, but Paula Wright offered to show her a few things she could begin on. Dixie went with Marcella to church there on Sunday, and although it was strange to her, it was somehow comforting.

She sat with Marcella in her Sunday School class and heard things she had never heard before. Gradually, life changed for Dixie. She began to hope. Every day seemed to bring new discoveries, new opportunities.

She came to know the children who visited the library. Sometimes she read to them. Once, a two-year-old girl climbed onto Dixie's lap as Dixie sat reading to the children. She was surprised at her feelings toward the child, a tenderness she had not known before.

She found that small town folks were not hard to know, that most of them were willing to let the past be the past. She began to make friends and found herself invited to cookouts and parties. It was a new life, one that she could not have anticipated.

At a square dance in the community building one Saturday night, Ted Bates asked her to be his partner. He patiently taught her the steps, and soon they were dancing as well as any other couple. She was moved by his gentle manner and kind words. Before the evening was done, he had asked her to go to the movie in Cranfield with him the next Friday night. She was stunned by the invitation—a date with a law officer!–but she accepted.

All week she couldn't help wondering, What does he expect? Does he think I'm still a hooker? What's he looking for? She found it hard to trust it as a simple date.

Friday evening came, and he picked her up at her house. They chatted about ordinary things on the way to Cranfield, about her work at the library, the folks in town she had met, and how she liked her house.

"It's nice, now that Marcella helped me fix it up. Wanna buy it?"

"I might," he said, grinning, and did not explain his answer.

After the movie, they went to an ice cream store and had chocolate sodas. In civilian clothes, Ted seemed more relaxed, more approachable. Dixie felt like a teenager again, young and hopeful for the future. Bill Haley and the Comets were playing on the jukebox. She wished she had bobby socks on and could jitterbug with Ted right there. It seemed that all the intervening years had dropped away, that she was actually starting her life over. Feelings she had never felt before–hope, delight, trust–frightened her at first. She wondered if that was normal. Trusting anyone was new to her. But she determined to take it as far as it would go.

They dated all summer, she and Ted: movies, trips to Conger for ice cream, long summer evening walks, long talks in the swing on Dixie's front porch. The town's suspicion regarding her began to drop away.

Now that she and Ted were dating, folks spoke to her on the streets and in the stores. Slowly, she was being accepted as a Thornburg resident.

When the trees shed their autumn glory in mid-October, she and Ted walked among rustling leaves by Bode's Creek, and in the fields where meadowlarks sang and wild asters bloomed. Ted had become a true friend, one who never asked her for anything but friendship. Dixie found herself trusting him with thoughts and feelings she had never admitted to anyone, even to herself. And there at the edge of a wood under an ancient burr oak tree, with the late afternoon sun making everything amber, he kissed her and told her that he loved her, and asked her to marry him.

"Oh, Ted! Are you sure you want someone like me?"

"Darlin', there's no one else like you. You're exactly the one I want," he said.

"But you don't really know me! If you knew . . ."

He put his hand over her mouth and said, "I know you're a woman who's had some rough ways to travel over, but you've pulled yourself together. You've let the beauty inside of you come out. You haven't allowed your past to govern who you are. And you've handled the busybodies in town with real class! I admire that, and I don't want to be without you."

She searched his face for any hint of deception and found herself trusting him, loving him with all her being. Was it really possible to be loved for herself alone? If she was ever to know, this was her chance. She threw her arms around his neck.

"Oh, yes! Yes, yes, yes!"

They were married the day before Thanksgiving in the Christian Church. All the friends she had made in town attended. Marcella stood up with her, and Ted's brother from Plainfield came to stand with him. The reception was beautiful: the ladies of the church had decorated the fellowship room downstairs in autumn colors, and Spencer's Bakery had baked a simple but beautiful wedding cake decorated with orange and yellow icing leaves.

The day after Thanksgiving the couple left for a short honeymoon. Ted felt obligated to be on the job most of the week. On Tuesday, with the help of friends, they moved Ted's things from his apartment into the house on Wood Street, and it was home.

Over the winter months, friends came frequently to visit. The Bateses were regular worshipers at the Christian Church. As the months passed and she made new friends, Dixie began to realize that life is a journey with many turnings, and at those turnings we meet people who need us, and we need them.

On Christmas Eve, she gave her husband the first sampler she had made with the guidance of Paula Wright.

"We can hang it over the bed," she told him.

It said simply, "God gave us each other to love."